D1014186
Mystery
of the
Secret Dolls

Other Apple Paperbacks
you will enjoy:

*Jamie and the Mystery Quilt*
by Vicki Berger Erwin

*Midnight in the Dollhouse*
by Marjorie Filley Stover

*A Ghost in the House*
by Betty Ren Wright

*Tales From Academy Street*
by Martha Derman

*Afternoon of the Elves*
by Janet Taylor Lisle

*The Daffodils*
by Christi Killien

# Mystery of the Secret Dolls

Vicki Berger Erwin

AN
**APPLE**
PAPERBACK

SCHOLASTIC INC.
New York Toronto London Auckland Sydney

ISBN 0-590-44412-3



12 11 10 9 8 7 6 5 4 5 6 7 8/9

Printed in the U.S.A. 40

First Scholastic printing, May 1993

*To my dad, Morgan Berger, who had the good fortune to be born into a wonderful, extended family and who shared that experience with me.*

*With thanks to my cousin, Connie White, for the memorable summers we spent together in her house beside the cemetery.*

# Mystery of the Secret Dolls

# 1

The bus jerked to a stop and roused Bonnie out of her slumber. She glanced out the window. The driver was unloading suitcases from the compartment in the side of the bus directly below her.

Bonnie tried to find her place in the book she had been reading before she dozed off.

The driver stuck his head inside the bus. "Callaway, young lady," he said to Bonnie.

She snapped her book shut and leaned out the window for a second look. Those were *her* bags he had put out on the sidewalk.

Bonnie stood up and quickly stuffed the remains of her bus ride into her backpack — the book, a couple of candy bar wrappers, and an empty soda can. She was glad her mom wasn't along to see what she had eaten for lunch.

Flipping her long, dark braid over her shoulder, Bonnie took a deep breath. She climbed down the three steps leading from the bus to the sidewalk, her head held high and her palms sweating.

Bonnie's eyes darted right, then left, trying to pick her aunts out of the four or five people walking by the bus. None of them looked near old enough to be her great-aunts, and no one made any move toward her as she paused on the bottom step, still holding on to the bus rail.

Bonnie swallowed. "This is the bus station?" she asked the driver.

He nodded as he slammed the luggage compartment door closed.

"But it says 'Restaurant. Country Kitchen Restaurant,' " Bonnie said. Her aunts had said they would meet her at the *bus station.*

"Bus station, too," the driver answered.

A woman who had been sitting in the back of the bus was standing on the step above Bonnie, tapping her foot impatiently.

"Do I have time to use the ladies' room?" the woman asked the driver.

"If you hurry," he replied.

"Excuse me, miss . . ." the woman began.

Bonnie jumped down to the sidewalk and joined the bus driver before the woman could finish.

"This all your stuff?" The driver tilted his head toward her suitcases.

"Yes, but . . ."

He took hold of the railing and pulled himself up the three steps in one smooth move.

"My aunts aren't here," Bonnie said to his back.

The driver looked at his watch, then shrugged. "Phone inside the restaurant."

Bonnie's shoulders slumped. She looked at the restaurant out of the corner of her eye. The front screen door was propped open. A line of men wearing T-shirts, jeans, and even a couple of men in overalls, sat on the stools along the counter. Most of them had on baseball-type caps with names like Caterpillar, John Deere, and Peterbilt on the fronts. The phone was hanging on the very back wall. Bonnie decided to wait a little longer to see if her aunts would show up.

As soon as the woman returned from the rest room and climbed onto the bus, the doors swooshed shut. The driver saluted Bonnie and pulled away.

She watched until the bus disappeared down the road, then sat down on the bench in front of the restaurant/bus station and took a look around at the town where she would be spending a good part of her summer.

The restaurant was located on one of the corners of a four-way stop. Across the street was a laundromat; catty-corner was a variety store — a real five-and-dime; and across from that a long, empty building with one sign that had FOR SALE OR LEASE on it, and a second one that announced AUCTION HERE EVERY WEDNESDAY, 6 P.M. A large, white banner stretched between the restaurant and the auction house and proclaimed in red letters:

COUNTY FAIR
JULY 27–30
FUN FOR ALL!

They still had a county fair? Bonnie's dad always talked about the Callaway County fairs that Aunt Nell and Aunt Mollie had taken him to every summer when he was a kid. Neither one of the aunts had any children of their own, so they used to invite nieces and nephews to visit. The fair had rides, games, music, and cooking contests that Aunt Mollie always won. If things worked out the way the aunts planned, Bonnie would still be in town for the fair. She wondered if they would take her.

If it stayed as hot as it was today, Bonnie didn't know if she'd even want to go. She lifted her braid off her neck. The heat was terrible! Her new top was soaked with sweat. Bonnie let her hair fall and pulled the shirt away from her back. She twisted to inspect the bench. She didn't want to ruin her clothes by getting country muck all over them.

"Hi!"

Bonnie let go of her shirt quickly and turned around. She had to shade her eyes with one hand to see who had spoken to her. The late afternoon sun was directly in front of her and made it almost impossible to make out any details about the person, but she was sure it wasn't either of her aunts.

Suddenly every word her mother had ever said about not speaking to strangers came back to Bonnie. She clutched her backpack with one hand and a slat of the bench with her other. Bonnie looked around for other people. No one was nearby except the farmers inside the restaurant. She looked down at the sidewalk.

As soon as her eyes recovered from the strong sunlight, Bonnie peeked again. It was a boy and he looked like he was about her age. Surely Mom would have no objections to her talking to a boy.

He plopped down on the bench and put one arm along the back. *"Parlez-vous Français? Habla Español? Sprechen Sie Deutsch?"* he asked.

Bonnie tried not to smile. His accent was terrible — he used the same for each language!

"I don't speak any other language, but I *know* you don't live here in Callaway."

"How do you know that?" Bonnie couldn't help but ask over the echo of her mother's voice in her head reminding her not to talk to just anybody.

He grinned. "I was right! You *aren't* from here.

You don't have any trace of a southern accent!"

"Neither do you," Bonnie said. "So how do you know I didn't just move to town?"

"Did you?" he asked.

Bonnie smiled and shook her head.

"So, where are you from?" the boy asked.

"St. Louis, I'm visiting my great-aunts. They're supposed to pick me up any minute."

"I thought you might be Bonnie," the boy said. He folded his arms across his chest and smiled.

Bonnie thought he looked very smug. It irritated her that he knew who she was when she had no idea at all who he was.

"You're all Mrs. Boone and Mrs. Snyder have talked about for the last week."

"You know Aunt Nell and Aunt Mollie?" Bonnie allowed herself to ask.

"Everyone knows Nell Boone," the boy said. "She's famous for those dolls she makes."

So where was she? Bonnie wondered. She'd worried for days something like this would happen. Left alone at a bus stop in a strange town. Her head started to pound and her stomach quivered.

"Everyone around here knows Mrs. Snyder, too. She's a dynamite cook. I'd be willing to mow their yard just for a piece of her chocolate cake."

The mention of her Aunt Mollie's cooking

piqued Bonnie's interest. Bonnie loved to cook. And eat, too. Without really thinking about it, she sucked in her stomach.

"Aunt Mollie has a restaurant, right?" Bonnie looked over her shoulder. *Was it the Country Kitchen Restaurant and Bus Stop?* she wondered.

The boy shook his head. "She used to. I guess she's too busy with the doll museum now. The restaurant closed last month."

Bonnie felt a stab of disappointment. She'd been invited to help her Aunt Nell with the doll museum, but what she'd really been looking forward to was the restaurant. She stared down at her hands.

"Hey, what's wrong?" the boy asked. "I swear I'm an okay guy. My name is Marc Allen and I'm here for the summer visiting my grandfather. We live right across the road from your aunts. I mow their yard and I'm helping with some of the fixing up at the museum."

Bonnie looked at Marc again. He seemed nice enough. He had dark, curly hair that was plastered wetly to his head, blue eyes, and, of all things, curly eyebrows. He was thin, like she wished *she* was. And he looked the kind of thin that could eat an entire chocolate cake and stay that way.

The only problem Bonnie had with his looks was

what he was wearing — a smelly, sweat-soaked T-shirt, gym shorts, and dirty socks with worn Nike running shoes.

"I've been working out," Marc explained as Bonnie's eyes came to rest on the sweat stains on his shirt. "Trying to get in shape for cross-country next fall."

"In this heat?" she said. "I hate to run."

"It's what I'm good at," said Marc.

"Where do you usually live?" Bonnie asked.

"Lots of places," he said, smiling. "My dad's in the army. He's in school this summer and won't be assigned a permanent duty station until August. I decided I'd rather be here than in an apartment on an army base where I didn't know anyone. There're lots of good places to run here. You can run for miles down some of the roads and not see another person. It beats a track any day."

"I don't know anybody here," Bonnie said. "I don't even know my aunts really. My dad said I'd met them once or twice when I was little, but I don't remember them. He used to always spend summers here."

Marc laughed. "You'll know everyone soon enough. People are pretty friendly around here. So, are you going to help with the museum, too?"

Bonnie sighed. "Well actually, I'm supposed to be working on a special enrichment project on family history for school. I called to ask Aunt Mollie a question and the next thing I knew I was on a bus on my way here. Aunt Nell said helping her with the museum would answer all my questions. And I didn't even call Aunt Nell. I called Aunt Mollie! My project is supposed to be a book of family recipes."

They sat in silence for a few minutes.

"I wish Aunt Nell or Aunt Mollie would hurry up and get here!" Bonnie burst out.

"They probably got busy and couldn't get away. It's only a few blocks to their house. You could walk," said Marc. "Just go down across the railroad track and past that feed mill. See it?"

Bonnie looked in the direction he pointed. She shaded her eyes with her hand again and nodded.

"Keep going, and the road curves. A gravel road goes off to the right. Where the road curves you'll see a kind of small stone building. That's your aunts' doll museum or soon-to-be doll museum. Check there first.

"If they're not there, the big, white house right behind it is where they live. You can't miss it."

Bonnie stood up and slung her backpack over her shoulder. Then she remembered her suitcases lined up against the wall. She sat back down.

"I'll never be able to carry all my suitcases even if it's only a little way," she said. Her eyes started to feel all prickly, like she was going to cry.

"My grandfather's office is right down the street. I'll take the suitcases there and we'll drop them off at your aunts' later."

Bonnie looked at her suitcases then at Marc. She tried to think of an alternative, but the thought that a five minute walk would have her at her aunts' overshadowed everything else. Besides, Marc seemed like someone she could trust. She stood up again.

"Okay," she agreed slowly.

"Listen, this isn't St. Louis," Marc said. "I'll bet you even if your aunts aren't at home, the door will be unlocked. You could probably even leave the suitcases here and come back and get them later. . . ."

"No! You take them, please," Bonnie interrupted.

"No problem."

Bonnie looked toward the grain mill silo. "Just go past that and to the curve?"

"You can't miss it."

"Thanks," she said to Marc.

Bonnie walked fast. She kept her eyes straight ahead, searching for the curve. She crossed the railroad track and passed the grain mill. Beyond the mill, she saw a small diner on the opposite side of the street. It had MOLLIE'S painted across the window in big red letters trimmed in white. A CLOSED sign hung on the door.

Bonnie crossed the street and peeked inside the restaurant window. The chairs were upside down on the tables, with their legs in the air. Red and white checked gingham curtains hung limply at the windows.

Bonnie's stomach growled. It was getting close to dinnertime. She could almost smell the hamburgers frying and the pies baking. Dad had told her all about how wonderful his aunt Mollie's cooking was. So why was the restaurant closed?

Behind her, someone gunned a car engine. Maybe it was the aunts. Bonnie turned around quickly, a big smile on her face.

A yellow Pontiac Trans Am, pitted with rust spots, had pulled up to the curb. Two teenaged boys were sitting in the front, cigarettes dangling out of their mouths. Bonnie looked to see if Marc was still standing outside the bus station. She didn't see him or anyone else on the street.

Bonnie flattened herself against the wall of the restaurant.

The boy sitting in the passenger seat leaned out of the window. He took his cigarette out of his mouth and blew out a stream of smoke. "Hey kid, you need a ride?" he asked.

Bonnie shook her head.

The boy threw the cigarette butt at her feet.

He said something she couldn't hear to the driver, then they both laughed. They took off their baseball caps and waved them toward her, as the car peeled away from the curb and raised a cloud of dust.

Bonnie started walking even faster. Those two looked like they were up to no good.

The road started to curve. Ahead, the small stone building appeared. A large, white frame house loomed behind it.

She ran across the road and up to the museum. The front door hung open.

"Aunt Nell? Aunt Mollie?" Bonnie called out, taking one step inside.

The museum was completely silent.

Bonnie took one more step. "Aunt Nell? Aunt Mollie?" she said again.

Still no one answered.

"Hello?" Bonnie said. "Anyone here?" She pushed the door open a little wider.

In the middle of the floor, a table lay on its side, one leg collapsed, and dolls were scattered all around.

Bonnie walked inside slowly and squatted down to pick up one of the dolls.

A dark reddish-brown smear stained the floor nearby.

Bonnie swallowed the hot liquid that surged

into her throat. She backed away unable to take her eyes off the blood.

The door pressed into her back. Bonnie gripped the knob, then whirled around and slammed the door shut behind her. She ran toward her aunts' house.

# 2

Bonnie practically flew up the steps to the porch. She beat on the front door.

When no one answered, she fumbled with the knob and the door swung inward.

Hesitating only a moment before entering, Bonnie stepped over the threshold into a large entry hall.

"Aunt Nell! Aunt Mollie!" she yelled. "Anybody!"

She took a few more steps inside and looked around, hoping to find a telephone.

A staircase to Bonnie's left curved up to a landing that stretched above the entire hallway where she stood. Beyond the stairs, an arched doorway led to a shadowed room. Stretching directly ahead was a dark, narrow hallway. A large rectangular doorway framed a shadowy room to her right. Bonnie turned in its direction and paused at the entryway as her eyes moved over the room.

It was a living room. The furniture was old. It wasn't particularly worn or even faded, but it looked like the stuff Bonnie saw in antique shops she visited with her mom or the museums her dad insisted on taking her to see.

The room was very large. Bonnie's footsteps echoed as she moved across the polished wood floor to stand in front of the portrait hanging over the stone fireplace.

The man in the picture had a trim beard and mustache, dark but tinged with gray. He was dressed in a gray military uniform with the letters C.S.A. on the shoulders, and Bonnie would swear he was glaring down at her.

She tried to swallow the lump in her throat. She moved backward, unable to break the hold that the soldier's cold, blue eyes had on her.

"Don't look at me like that," Bonnie said under her breath.

She whirled around and ran straight into a tall, black girl.

Both of them screamed.

Bonnie backed away. She wasn't in the right house. How embarrassing! She couldn't even follow the simple directions Marc had given her. What could she possibly say to this girl to explain why she was in her house?

"I was just down at the museum," Bonnie blurted out. "Everything is scattered and there's bl-blood on the floor. I came up here because I thought this was my aunts' house."

"Bonnie?" the girl asked.

Bonnie nodded.

"You're in the right house," the girl quickly assured her.

"Then where is everyone? Where is Aunt Nell? Why didn't they meet me at the bus station? Who are you?" Bonnie asked all the questions without even taking a breath.

The girl sighed loudly. "We had to take Mrs. Boone to the doctor's. She fell. Your aunts will be here in a minute and they'll tell you all about it. Mrs. Snyder's having trouble getting Mrs. Boone to ride in the wheelchair." She walked toward the hall.

Bonnie hurried after her. She didn't want to be left alone until she knew more about what was going on. "A wheelchair? My dad didn't say anything about Aunt Nell being in a wheelchair," she said to the girl's back.

"Welcome to Little Dixie," a voice said, not unpleasantly, from the porch.

The girl pushed the screen door open.

Bonnie could see a small, gray-haired woman sitting in a wheelchair outside on the porch.

"Here, hold this." The girl motioned for Bonnie to hold the screen open. She stepped outside and pushed the chair past Bonnie. Another older woman followed, giving constant instructions.

"Now don't pull the chair back too far, Lynette. It might make Nell dizzy, what with that bump on her head. And watch the doorways. You don't want to accidentally bump her leg. . . ."

"For heaven's sake, Mollie, hush up! If you don't like the way Lynette is pushing me, *you* do it," the woman in the wheelchair said.

Bonnie watched her Aunt Mollie press her lips firmly together. The woman's face turned an even deeper red than it already was.

The woman who, by process of elimination, had to be Aunt Nell turned to Bonnie and looked her over carefully.

"I hope living in the city hasn't turned you into a Yankee," she said without even a hint of a smile.

"Aunt Nell?" Bonnie asked.

"Of course. Who else would be sitting here in *my* house in a contraption like this?" she answered.

One of her aunt's legs was extended, wrapped from knee to toe in a white cast. A large bandage covered one side of her head.

"What happened?" asked Bonnie.

"A little spill, that's all," her aunt answered.

"More than that," Aunt Mollie contradicted. "Her leg is broken and she had to have six stitches over her eye. We had to go all the way over to Audrain to the hospital. Doctor Allen couldn't even fix her up in his office."

"What happened?" Bonnie asked again, feeling overwhelmed by the situation — new place, new people, a wheelchair, blood. . . .

"This morning, over at the museum, I climbed up on a table, just like I've done a hundred times before, to change a light bulb, and the darn thing collapsed," said Aunt Nell.

"I was just over at the museum. I saw the dolls all over the floor and the blood," said Bonnie. "Maybe I'd better call Dad."

"Whatever for?" Aunt Nell asked gruffly.

"He could come to get me," said Bonnie.

"Whatever for?" Aunt Nell asked again.

"Surely you don't want me here now!"

"Want you? It's not a question of wanting you. I need a pair of young legs now more than ever."

"But Aunt Nell . . ." Bonnie began.

"We can take care of you just fine," the girl named Lynette said to Aunt Nell.

Aunt Nell patted the girl's hand and smiled at her.

Bonnie wondered who on earth this girl, Lynette, was. Already she could see that Aunt Nell thought Lynette was special. She'd actually smiled at her.

"You and Mollie have plenty to do around here without worrying about me. I need Bonnie. Bonnie's family," Aunt Nell said firmly.

"All right, Nell, what does that make *me*?" asked Aunt Mollie, still standing behind the wheelchair.

"Mollie . . ." Aunt Nell began, then turned to Bonnie. "Where are our manners? We didn't even bother to introduce ourselves. Bonnie, this is your great-aunt Mollie, my little sister."

"I'm pleased to meet you," Bonnie said, even though it sounded awfully formal to her ears.

"I'm so glad you decided to visit," Aunt Mollie said. "For a while there it seemed like we ran out of young nieces and nephews with time to visit their old aunts. We haven't even seen that dad of yours for a while, and *he* keeps in touch better than most. We could use a little life around here. And heaven knows, Lynette should be glad to see you. She must be sick to death of sitting around here with us old women." As Aunt Mollie talked, she moved toward Bonnie, threw her arms around her, hugging her tightly, then kissed her soundly on the forehead.

Bonnie tried to pull away, but Aunt Mollie kept one arm tightly about her shoulders.

Bonnie found it hard to believe that the two women before her were sisters. Aunt Nell was so tiny and immaculate looking, even in bandages.

Her hair glowed with a silvery tint and she wore a tailored skirt and blouse.

On the other hand, Aunt Mollie was . . . Bonnie could think of no kinder word than large, perhaps even extra-large. She wore a brightly colored, floral print shirt and bright green slacks. Her hair was a peculiar shade of gold. Aunt Mollie wore jewelry, lots of clinking, clanking, jangling jewelry. And she smelled as flowery as her shirt looked.

"By the way, this is *my* house, too," Aunt Mollie said to Bonnie. "Although you wouldn't know it from talking to my sister. Daddy left it to *both* of us. Nell's lived here her whole entire life, even when she was married. Now me, I moved away with my husband and didn't come back until he passed away. That was about the same time Nell's husband died. Thought we could be company for each other. Shoulda known all we'd do was fight. That's the way it's always been. Now she doesn't even want to admit I'm part of the family!"

"Now, Mollie, that isn't true. I just meant that you're no use at all when it comes to helping with the dolls. Besides, you have enough to do with setting up the books and getting the volunteers organized. Bonnie can help me with the real work."

Bonnie felt Aunt Mollie stiffen. She squeezed

Bonnie's shoulders tightly once more, then abruptly let go of her.

Throughout the entire discussion, Lynette stood to one side, not saying a word.

"We'd better get you into bed," Aunt Mollie said, turning Aunt Nell's wheelchair.

"Bed, schmed," Aunt Nell grumbled as Aunt Mollie pushed her through an arch to the left of the entry hall. Lynette followed them.

Bonnie flopped on the bottom step of the staircase. She stuck the end of her braid in her mouth and started chewing.

She would call her mom and dad anyway, she decided, just to let them know what was going on. Maybe they would insist she come home.

*Not likely*, Bonnie thought. Her mom had decided that since Bonnie was going to be gone for a part of the summer, she would go visit an old college friend who had moved to California. She wouldn't be happy about changing those plans now. And Bonnie didn't want her to have to. But they should know.

*Where would the phone be?* Bonnie wondered.

"Bonnie! I need to talk to you. Bonnie!" Aunt Nell sounded agitated.

Bonnie walked under the arch and entered a room brightened by the setting sun. She blinked rapidly as her eyes adjusted to the change in the light. Bonnie had the impression that the room was filled with people. She saw eyes everywhere. However, as the room came into focus, she realized it was filled with dolls — every type of doll imaginable.

Bonnie stopped beside a table and picked up a bald baby doll. It looked so real! She cradled it in her arms and stroked the face. It was smooth and silky. The baby even smelled powdery.

Bonnie laid the baby down gently.

She touched the silk gown of a doll balanced on a stand. It looked like it was about to step off and walk down the aisle of a church to the strains of "The Wedding March."

Bonnie turned and crossed the room. A large doll dressed in a tartan kilt held bagpipes poised to play. Next to the piper, Queen Elizabeth posed, crown and all.

A gray uniform caught Bonnie's eye. She picked up the doll and found herself staring into the same blue eyes she had faced earlier in the portrait in the living room.

"That's your great-great-great-grandfather, Colonel Seth Scott, Confederate States of America," Aunt Nell said.

Bonnie turned. C.S.A., Confederate States of America. That's what the letters on the uniform meant. Her great-grandfather had been a rebel and fought against the Union during the Civil War. The information Bonnie needed for her project was just falling into her lap.

Her aunt Nell was propped up on a daybed in an adjoining room.

Aunt Mollie and Lynette were busy trying to figure out how to collapse the wheelchair.

"I use these two rooms as my studio," Aunt Nell said. "My bedroom is upstairs, but I think I'd rather be down here until I can maneuver a bit easier."

Bonnie twisted her braid.

"Come here, girl. Let me get a good look at you."

Bonnie walked over to the bed and stood there quietly.

"Did I introduce you to Lynette?" Aunt Nell asked, fluttering her hands in the direction of the young, black girl. "Aunt Mollie and I thought it would be more fun for you if you had someone around closer to your age. It worked out just perfectly that Lynette's mom had to go out of town this week to some kind of computer training for the bank she works for. She was going to get someone to come in and stay with Lynette, but we invited her to stay here with us.

"Lynette's grandma used to work for me. I've known this girl ever since she was born. They live right down the road a piece. And Lynette shares an interest in my babies." Aunt Nell smiled at Lynette again and winked.

Lynette sidestepped closer to Aunt Nell's bed.

The wheelchair had finally given up its fight. Aunt Mollie was now trying to get it to stay tucked away behind the door leading to another hallway.

Aunt Nell reached over and pulled Lynette down to sit beside her on the edge of the bed.

Bonnie smiled at Lynette. The girl was so pretty and she looked older than twelve! She was much taller than Bonnie, slender, and wore a plain white T-shirt with denim shorts. Her black hair was pulled straight back, framing an oval face. Her skin glowed a deep, warm brown.

However, from the expression Lynette wore everytime she looked at her, Bonnie doubted that Aunt Nell's plan to provide her with an instant friend was going to work.

"I think you two girls will get along fine," said Aunt Mollie.

"What do you think?" Aunt Nell asked.

"About what?" asked Bonnie. She didn't think Aunt Nell would like to hear what she thought about the chances for a friendship between her and Lynette.

"The dolls!" Aunt Nell said.

"They're . . . they're . . . they're so many," said Bonnie.

Her aunt frowned.

"I mean, they're wonderful," Bonnie rushed to amend, "but there are just so many."

"That's why I decided to open the museum. The Scott women have been making dolls for almost one hundred fifty years."

"Not all of them," Aunt Mollie interrupted.

Aunt Nell quieted her sister with a glare. "Many of the dolls were on commission, but we've kept our share.

"And we have all of the family dolls. You know about those don't you?"

Bonnie shook her head.

Her aunt frowned again. "You saw the portrait of your great-grandfather in there?" She pointed toward the living room.

Bonnie nodded.

"Now look down at that doll you're holding," said Aunt Nell.

Bonnie looked.

"We have a portrait doll like that for every member of our family. Those alone would almost fill a small museum. We've also recovered a number of dolls that were commissioned over the years. They'll all be on display, too.

"The museum is scheduled to open August 3. I mean, it *will* open August 3," her aunt said.

"Nell," Aunt Mollie broke in, "maybe you'd better postpone the opening. The fire, the break-in, the broken windows, and now your fall. . . .”

Lynette stood up and walked over to the window. She stared outside as the conversation continued.

“I can’t postpone it! The invitations have gone out. Too many people have made plans to attend. Important people, Mollie, who can’t rearrange their schedules to accommodate a clumsy, old woman.”

“Aunt Nell, what fire? What break-in are you talking about? I don’t understand.” Bonnie felt like she had walked in on the middle of a movie as she struggled to comprehend what was going on.

“We’ve had a few mishaps down at the museum. Nothing to worry about and nothing that’s going to stop me,” Aunt Nell said firmly.

“There was a small fire in the building right after we announced we were opening the museum — deliberately set, the fire chief himself said so. Then after we got that all cleaned up, someone broke all the windows out and got inside. They spray painted all over the floors and walls. We had to put down a whole new floor,” Aunt Mollie explained in her fast, breathless way.

“I’m sure my fall had nothing to do with those other pranks,” Aunt Nell said.

"That table was perfectly fine yesterday," Aunt Mollie said.

"Why would anyone want to break into a doll museum?" Bonnie asked.

"Someone obviously doesn't want the museum to open. Some *Yankee.*" Aunt Nell spit out the word like it tasted bad.

"Nell, you need to settle down and get some rest." Aunt Mollie patted her sister's cast.

"Rest! How can I rest when someone might be down in my museum right now doing who knows what?" Aunt Nell said.

"What about the security system? When are they going to install it? Mollie, you need to call them again," said Aunt Nell. "Who would have ever thought I'd need a security system here in Callaway?"

"Why do you need a security system for a doll museum?" Bonnie asked.

No one answered Bonnie.

"I called. They said they'd get to it as soon as possible," Aunt Mollie said as she rummaged in a large straw bag she had slung over her shoulder. "Where is that key?"

"The door is unlocked?" Aunt Nell asked, almost shrieking.

"When I saw you there in a heap on the floor, the last thing on my mind was locking the door behind us. But don't worry, I'm going to go take care of that right now," said Aunt Mollie.

Lynette opened a desk drawer and handed Aunt Mollie a large iron key.

Aunt Mollie hurried out.

And Aunt Nell visibly relaxed. She asked quite pleasantly, "Did you know that the museum building once housed a doll factory of sorts? It belonged to Margaret Scott, the first serious doll maker in the family. Although she never called it a factory — always a studio. It predates the Civil War. We've lived here, in Callaway and in this house, since the 1850s. The colonel packed up and moved here from Virginia before the War Between the States. This is the sort of information you need for your project, right?"

"Yes, but I don't need it right now," Bonnie said. "You should be resting. . . ."

"The colonel brought his wife, his two daughters, his son . . ."

"She's right. You *should* be resting," Lynette said.

"The museum is almost ready," Aunt Nell continued. "All we have to do is some more cleaning up, slap a little paint around, set up the displays. You can do that and work on your family history project at the same time. They're practically the same thing."

"I don't know," Bonnie answered. "What about

Lynette and Aunt Mollie? They know a lot more about dolls than I do." She looked down at the doll she was holding.

"Lynette will certainly help, but I want you to pitch in, too. This could all belong to you someday," Aunt Nell said. "As for Mollie, what she knows about dolls you could write on the head of a pin. It's all I can do to keep her out of the kitchen long enough to get anything accomplished."

"What about Aunt Mollie's restaurant?" Bonnie asked. "I walked past it on my way here. Why isn't it open? Dad talks about what a good cook she is all the time."

"That! Doomed from the start. It takes more to run a restaurant than a few good recipes, but you can't tell Mollie a thing. She had to find out the hard way," said Aunt Nell.

"She is a good cook," said Lynette.

"I don't dispute that," Aunt Nell admitted, "but she has no business sense at all. I finally had to put a stop to it. She was just frittering away her inheritance on that restaurant. I had to stop her before she used the money I'd counted on for the museum.

"I told her we could add a little snack bar onto the museum. People might want a bite to eat after looking at my dolls — um, *our* dolls."

Bonnie wished she had a little snack right now. She wondered if Aunt Mollie had anything in the kitchen. Most of all she wanted to try one of Aunt Mollie's donuts. Her dad said she made them from scratch. That was definitely one of the recipes she wanted to include in her cookbook. If she did a cookbook.

Bonnie couldn't deny the dolls exerted a strange pull on her. She'd never had many dolls, a Barbie when she was younger and a baby doll or two. She'd never really wanted a doll, but now Bonnie itched to look at every single one of her aunts' dolls. They *would* make an interesting project.

Bonnie laid her "grandfather" down and picked up the doll nearest her, a perfectly turned out hoopskirted belle. She turned back the skirt and marvelled at the tiny hoop. The costume was complete down to lace trim on the pantalets.

"The colonel's wife," her aunt said.

Bonnie put her down quickly. It made her feel weird. The doll was so real-looking she felt like she was actually looking at her grandmother's underwear.

"Lynette, why don't you take Bonnie up and show her to her room," directed Aunt Nell. "I need to rest. We have lots of work to do."

# 3

Lynette walked past Bonnie, then paused in the archway. "Aren't you coming?" she asked.

Bonnie hurried after her. "It's so hot in here," she said, trying to make conversation. "Isn't the air-conditioning working?"

"Air-conditioning?" Lynette gave a short laugh. "We don't have air-conditioning. You're in the country, girl. We have all this fresh country air blowing around free for the asking."

No air-conditioning! Bonnie immediately felt even hotter.

"You ready to go to your room?" Lynette asked.

"Lead on," said Bonnie, trying to be agreeable.

"Are these your suitcases?" Lynette pointed at two bags sitting beside the front door.

"How did they get there?" Bonnie asked.

Lynette shrugged.

A book rested on top of one of the suitcases.

Bonnie picked it up. The cover showed some kind of gray stone statue of a horse.

Before she could open the book, Lynette lifted it out of her hands.

"Where'd you get this?" she asked.

"It's not mine," Bonnie answered. "It was just here."

"If your aunt . . ."

A piece of paper fluttered out of the book and landed on the floor at Bonnie's feet. She moved quickly to pick it up.

Bonnie unfolded the paper and read: "This should help you with your project. I'll drop by tomorrow. Marc."

"Marc must have dropped off my suitcases, like he promised he would," Bonnie said. "And he says the book will help me with my project."

"Marc? Marc Allen?" said Lynette.

Bonnie nodded. "I met him at the bus station."

"You know Dr. Allen's grandson? You sure do get around fast." Lynette handed her the book. "Did he tell you his grandfather was a Yankee?"

Bonnie sighed. She was so tired, so hot, so confused. She slung her backpack over her shoulder and picked up one of her suitcases. "Why does everybody here keep talking about Yankees? What does it mean?" Bonnie asked.

"It's one of Mrs. Boone's words. To her, it

means anybody who's doing something she doesn't approve of," said Lynette. "It's probably one of those things that got passed down along with the dolls. You saw your great-grandfather Seth in his Confederate uniform. He fought against the Yankees in the War Between the States and sometimes it's like the Scotts never got over that loss." Lynette picked up the other suitcase and started up the stairs.

Bonnie followed.

"Why doesn't Aunt Nell approve of Dr. Allen?" Bonnie asked.

"Mrs. Boone doesn't disapprove of Dr. Allen as a person. She just doesn't agree with his interpretation of the Civil War," Lynette said.

They reached the landing. Straight ahead, several steps led up to a door.

"That door goes out to the porch that runs all along the second floor. You can get to the porch from your room, too," Lynette said.

"Your aunt Nell usually sleeps in the room over there." She pointed to the doorway on the right.

Lynette opened one of two doors on the left side of the hallway, then stood aside and waited for Bonnie to go in first.

Bonnie could see nothing but shadows in the room. She shivered in spite of the heat. "Where's the light switch?"

Lynette groped along the wall inside the door. Bonnie heard a click and the shadows disappeared.

The room smelled like it hadn't been used in a long time. The first thing she did was to cross the room to raise the shades and throw open all the windows.

Lynette tossed the suitcase she had carried upstairs on the bed. She opened a door. "Here's the porch. You could sleep out there if it gets too hot."

Bonnie couldn't imagine it getting any hotter. She hoisted her suitcase onto the bed, dropped her backpack on the floor, and tossed the book Marc had given her on a bedside table.

Lynette retrieved the book and started flipping through it.

"Aunt Nell must approve of Marc, though. He said he was helping with the museum," said Bonnie. She sat down on the bed. "So, Dr. Allen is a Yankee?" she asked.

Lynette looked up, surprised. "You could say that. He wrote this book. Take a look at this." She stuck the open book out to Bonnie. "There are a few things in here your aunt *didn't* tell you about the dolls."

Bonnie read the chapter title. "Callaway: Legend and Lore." She looked at the page but it didn't make much sense to her.

Lynette took the book back, turned a few pages, then held a picture out to Bonnie.

Bonnie looked at the picture of . . . a doll. She still wasn't sure what Lynette was trying to make her see.

"What your aunt didn't tell you is that in addition to his family, Colonel Seth Scott also brought five black slaves with him from Virginia. One of those slaves was selected because she was so valuable to the family doll business. I know because that woman was *my* great-great-great-grandmother, Rosa Scott," Lynette said. "She was so proud of the part she played in the dollmaking, she even kept the family's last name after she was freed, like a lot of slaves did back then."

Bonnie looked down at the book again. This time she realized what Lynette was referring to. The doll in the picture was black.

Lynette read aloud from the book:

> "Margaret Scott was one of the few dollmakers of her time to create black dolls. In an ironic twist, black dolls similar to those fashioned by Miss Scott began to appear whenever a slave from the area managed to escape to freedom. Legend had it that the dolls were a 'calling card' of the Underground Railroad. A

member of a staunchly Confederate family, Miss Scott ceased production of her black dolls after neighboring slaveowners complained.

Examples of Miss Scott's work turn up only rarely. They are prized by the collector and are worth a small fortune to the lucky finder.

The "calling card" dolls are easily distinguished both in refinement of style and by a small red heart sewed on the chest of the slave dolls.

"Not a word in there about the slaves involved in the doll making, is there?" Lynette asked when she finished reading.

"No, but it says the dolls are valuable. They're worth money?" Bonnie asked.

Lynette laughed. "Those dolls down in your aunt's studio are invaluable *and* irreplaceable," she said. "But, they are worth nothing compared to these dolls." Lynette poked her finger at the picture in the book. "Just wait until I find them. And I *will* find them!"

"Find them? What do you mean — find them?" Bonnie asked Lynette.

"Didn't you hear what I read? The dolls are rare, the book says. In fact I've only seen one of the dolls in my whole life. Your aunt keeps it locked up. It's that valuable. But my great-great-great-grandmother told my great-great-grandmother who told . . ."

"I get the picture," Bonnie said.

"Who told my mother who told me that they kept on making black dolls even after they had been ordered to stop.

"Dr. Allen leaves out that part. Margaret didn't decide to stop making the dolls herself. Her father ordered her to stop or he'd close down the entire doll-making operation."

Bonnie took the book and reread the passage about the dolls.

Then Lynette continued on. "My family has been involved in doll making down through the years, just like yours. Until my mom came along that is. She wants to be successful. To her, that means making lots of money. She works all the time. It didn't used to be so bad, before my grandma died. We lived with Grandma and she took care of me. Now, Mom hires someone or I come stay with Mrs. Boone. But I don't mind staying here. I came to work here with Grandma all the time anyway. I'd miss the dolls if I couldn't see them," said Lynette.

"Aunt Nell seems to do all right making dolls. I'd say she's successful," said Bonnie.

"That's because she has the *name*. We've always just worked for her. You know she wants to pass it all to you, don't you?" asked Lynette. She was watching Bonnie very carefully.

"I don't know why. We don't even know each other," said Bonnie. She suddenly realized what was bothering Lynette. "Do you want to make dolls?" she asked.

Lynette nodded slowly. She didn't look at Bonnie.

"Aunt Nell seems to like you a lot," said Bonnie.

"Like I said, Mrs. Boone lets me hang around. Sometimes she even lets me help, but I'm not family," Lynette said.

"Why would you want to be?" Bonnie asked. "Aunt Mollie is her sister and look how she treats her. I don't have any sisters or brothers — and I don't want any if that's the way they act."

"I guess I'm used to it. The way Mrs. Boone talks, that doesn't mean anything. She's always been like that. And Mrs. Snyder is always nice," said Lynette.

"I already figured that out," said Bonnie.

"That's not to say your aunt Nell isn't nice. She just makes me mad sometimes because she refuses to admit there are any more black dolls. Just wait until I find them, though. When I do, your aunt and everyone else around here will have to admit that my family played an important part in the history of Callaway, too."

Aunt Mollie suddenly appeared at the doorway. "Can I interrupt the girl talk for just a moment?" she asked.

"Come on in," said Bonnie.

"I thought you might be hungry." Aunt Mollie set a tray piled with sandwiches and a pitcher of lemonade on the dresser.

"Thank you. I'm really thirsty," said Bonnie, immediately pouring herself a glass of lemonade.

"How did you manage already to get a copy of *the book*?" asked Aunt Mollie.

"Marc Allen left it when he brought my suitcases."

"I was telling her about the black dolls," said Lynette.

"You just never give up, do you?" said Aunt Mollie to Lynette.

"What about you, Aunt Mollie? Do you think there are any hidden dolls someplace around here?" asked Bonnie.

"I've never seen any," Aunt Mollie said slowly.

"What about these dolls left as calling cards?" asked Bonnie.

"Those are totally different," said Lynette. "You read the book. They were probably left by the Underground Railroad. The Scotts were 'staunch Southerners,' hardly the types to be involved in helping slaves escape. They owned slaves. The Allens were the ones who were against slavery. They weren't only Yankees, they were abolitionists."

"But maybe your great-grandmother — "

"No way! She was a slave herself. Whoever ran the Railroad probably left the dolls as some kind of bad joke on the Scotts."

"Now Bonnie, don't let Lynette fill your head with all her crazy ideas about finding those dolls," said Aunt Mollie.

"I don't think it's crazy," Bonnie said. "It sounds exciting to me. I'd *like* to find them."

"You eat up and get some rest," said Aunt Mollie. "If any dolls are hiding around here after more than a hundred years, they'll still be here tomorrow." She gave Bonnie a kiss on the forehead and left the room.

"You need anything else?" Lynette asked.

"Will you be in the room next door?" Bonnie asked.

"That's what the plan was, but I think I'll sleep downstairs until your aunt gets better," said Lynette. "I wouldn't be able to hear her from up here if she needs anything in the night."

"What about Aunt Mollie? Where does she sleep?"

"She has her own set of rooms, upstairs, in back of the house. You have to go up the backstairs off of the hallway downstairs to get there," said Lynette.

Bonnie tried hard to think of something else to talk about. She wanted to ask Lynette all kinds of questions about this new place and all the new people and old people she was being bombarded with. And, she wasn't at all anxious to be left upstairs alone in a strange house.

"Whose room is this?" she asked finally.

"Nobody's now. I guess it's belonged to lots of people. It was your aunt Nell's room when she was a girl, and Margaret's, too. Margaret died in here all alone," Lynette said sadly.

Bonnie looked at the bed. Had she died *there*? she wondered, guiltily. "The Margaret who made all the dolls?" she asked.

"Yes — she was the first to become well-known for her portrait dolls. But she didn't do it all alone. She had slaves to help her."

"So Margaret painted that picture of the colonel and also made the doll of him?

Lynette nodded. "And maybe she'll visit you tonight," she said, smiling.

"Yeah, right," Bonnie said with a nervous laugh.

"Good night." Lynette gave a little wave from the doorway and walked out of the room.

Bonnie listened to the footsteps fade as Lynette descended the stairs.

"Okay, let her leave. I don't need to hear about ghosts anyway," Bonnie said, her voice sounding very loud in the empty room.

She picked up a sandwich and nibbled on it. It was tuna salad. She hated tuna. Bonnie returned it to the platter and began to unpack.

The dolls were *valuable*. Bonnie couldn't get over that fact. It repeated itself in her head over and over. No wonder someone tried to break into the museum. It wasn't anything personal, they just wanted the dolls.

She circled the room. It seemed even bigger now that she was alone. All the furniture in the room was old, just as it had been downstairs. Strange, Bonnie thought, that there are so many dolls downstairs, yet none here.

When she got to the door leading to the porch, Bonnie pushed it open.

She stepped outside and took a deep breath. The country smelled totally different from the city — a combination of honeysuckle and new-mown grass made even sweeter by the absence of the smell of car exhaust.

And it was quiet. Bonnie could hear herself breathe as well as hear all kinds of insects chirping together to form a rural chorus.

She looked up.

Bonnie would swear there were more stars in the sky above Callaway than in St. Louis. They lit up the sky, making it look like a dark blue blanket sprinkled with silver that she could reach up and pull around her — if she wasn't so hot.

The ground below seemed to stretch endlessly. A low stone wall divided the grounds.

Bonnie looked beyond the wall. She leaned over the railing and strained to make out the strange shapes that dotted the horizon.

Behind her, inside, Bonnie heard a creak, then another.

It's just an old house, she assured herself.

Bonnie turned back to the view off the porch. Suddenly she could pick out individual shapes.

They were tombstones! She was living right next door to a graveyard.

Bonnie heard a door slam close by.

"Aunt Nell?" she called into the inside darkness.

Silence answered her.

# 4

Bonnie hurried back inside her room. She pulled on the door to the porch firmly to make certain it was shut, then leaned against it to make doubly sure it was tightly closed.

Carefully looking into every corner of the room, Bonnie made sure no one had slipped into her room unannounced. Everything appeared to be just as she'd left it. Except that the door to the hallway was now closed.

For a moment, Bonnie didn't even breathe. Then she quickly realized a stray breeze must have caught the door and slammed it shut. Being here in this strange house was making her think strange thoughts. Aunt Nell with her broken leg was the last person who could have come into her room, and yet she was the first one Bonnie thought of.

She massaged her forehead right above her eyes. It wasn't that late, but she felt very tired.

Bonnie stretched her arms above her head, then peeled her shirt off and threw it across the room. She slipped out of her shorts and tossed them on top of her shirt. She kicked her shoes into the air and pulled her socks off, flinging them in the same direction as her shoes.

Bonnie pulled a T-shirt out of her suitcase and let it drop down over her head. It was so big it hung all the way to her knees.

In the adjoining bathroom, she splashed cool water over her face and hurriedly brushed her teeth.

Bonnie came out of the bathroom and dove onto the bed. She lay there on her stomach, trying to relax.

After a while, Bonnie sat up and pulled her legs, Indian-style, under her. The room looked better now, she decided as she looked around; more lived-in, more comfortable, more familiar.

Leaning across to the dresser, Bonnie picked up half a chicken salad sandwich and looked at it. She'd already brushed her teeth. But who would know? She ate it in five bites, then ate the other half and washed it down with some warm, watery lemonade. The bread tasted delicious, definitely homemade. She pulled the top slice off the tuna sandwich and ate it for dessert. The bread was almost as good as a cookie.

Bonnie got up and reopened the door leading to

the porch hoping to encourage a breeze through the room. She pulled back the quilt covering her bed and slipped between the cool white sheets. She shut her eyes.

The light was still on.

Bonnie sat up again. Tired as she was, she couldn't sleep. She pulled the book she had been reading on the bus out of her backpack. As she dropped the pack on the floor, it knocked against the table, rocking it. Bonnie heard something drop off the table and hit the floor.

She reached down and groped around under the bed. She felt a soft lump, grasped it, and pulled it upward.

As it emerged over the edge, Bonnie found herself looking down at . . . herself!

She was holding a doll which had a braid the same dark shade of brown as her own hair. Its eyes were the same blue. Freckles dotted its face. Even the mouth was shaped the same.

Bonnie stroked the doll's gown. The clothes weren't like hers at all. The doll wore a navy blue dress trimmed in lace, with a long, full skirt.

At second glance, the hair was different, too. The doll's braid was caught up in a net. Still, Bonnie couldn't escape the fact that the doll looked remarkably like her.

A streak of red caught her eye. A piece of white

paper with broad red letters was tucked under the doll's arm.

Bonnie pulled the paper out so she could read the words.

DON'T BELIEVE EVERYTHING YOU HEAR.

It was almost like a saying out of a Chinese fortune cookie.

*The note's not for me,* Bonnie tried to convince herself.

She set the doll back on the table and searched the room again. The doll had not been there before she went out on the porch. Bonnie specifically recalled noticing that there were no dolls in the room. The book about Callaway was the only thing on the table and it was still there. Someone had to have brought the doll in and left it.

Bonnie picked up the doll again. She moved slowly and quietly to the door to the hallway. She opened it slightly and listened through the crack. The hall sounded empty.

Bonnie scurried to the stairs and paused, gripping the rail. Very little moonlight seeped through the curtained windows to light the stairs.

The floor behind her creaked. Bonnie skimmed down the steps, looking over her shoulder. When the handrail gave out, Bonnie stepped out expecting to find the floor. Instead, she realized, there was one more step. She landed in a heap, her right ankle twisted under her.

"Who's there?" Aunt Nell's voice pierced the dark.

"It's me," Bonnie managed to say. "I missed the last step."

Her aunt didn't answer.

Bonnie stood up carefully, waiting until the last moment to put any weight on her right foot.

Pain shot upward, all the way to her stomach. Bonnie broke out in a cold sweat.

"You still there?" Aunt Nell asked.

"I've hurt my ankle," Bonnie said weakly.

"Come in here and let me see it."

Bonnie didn't know if she could make it into the studio. She hopped along, the doll tucked under her arm, holding onto the wall and then to the tables.

In Aunt Nell's room, only a small bedside light burned, leaving most of the room in shadows.

"What are you doing up, anyway?" Aunt Nell asked.

Bonnie held the doll up so her aunt could see it.

"Where did you get this?" her aunt demanded, her cheeks flushed.

"It was in my room," Bonnie said, finally reaching her aunt and sitting down on the edge of the bed.

"Your room!"

"I was out on the porch and heard a noise in my room. When I came back to bed the doll must have been on the table, because I knocked it off and found it under the bed."

"That's incredible. This doll has been missing for months. It must have gotten shoved under the bed somehow," Aunt Nell said. "Mollie should have found it when she cleaned."

"No, I heard it drop onto the floor when I went to put my backpack down. Someone must have come into my room and left it on the table beside the bed while I was out on the porch. And the doll was holding a note, too."

Bonnie tried to find the piece of paper. She must have dropped it when she fell, but Bonnie didn't feel like going back to see just yet. "The note said 'Don't believe everything you hear,' " she explained to her aunt.

"That's ridiculous! This doll couldn't have been on the table. You could have knocked anything on the floor," Aunt Nell said, "and then happened to grab hold of the doll when you went searching under the bed. The note, well, I don't see any connection between it and the doll. It must have been under the bed, too, and you picked it up with the doll."

"There wasn't anything but a book on that table," Bonnie insisted. She stood up to go get the note. Aunt Nell must be one of those people who had to see to believe. But as soon as Bonnie put weight on her ankle, she had to sit back down.

"It doesn't really matter *how* the doll got there. I'm just glad you found it," said Aunt Nell. She straightened the doll's clothing and hair.

"But I didn't find it," Bonnie said. "Someone brought the doll into my room. And I want to know who that person was."

"There aren't very many choices. I certainly didn't come upstairs. Mollie didn't, because I would have seen her come out of her room. And I imagine Lynette's asleep. I think the doll was there all the time," said Aunt Nell.

Bonnie didn't feel like arguing the point until she had the note to show her aunt. She changed tactics. "This doll looks just like me."

"It does, doesn't it?" Aunt Nell replied. "I should have noticed that. You do look like Margaret — although her mother must have had a fit about the freckles. Women just didn't expose themselves to the sun back then."

"That doll is Margaret?" Bonnie asked.

Aunt Nell nodded and handed it back to her niece.

"And I look like her," Bonnie said in almost a whisper.

"She was quite a woman for her time," Aunt Nell said.

Bonnie laid Margaret across her knees. "Can I sleep down here? I don't like it up there by myself. This house makes funny noises."

"And just where do you suppose you'd sleep?" Aunt Nell asked.

"Where's Lynette sleeping? I'll sleep with her."

"Then that's upstairs. She's in the room right next to yours."

Why did she lie about sleeping downstairs? Bonnie wondered. Unless it was to make her more nervous about being alone. She remembered how Lynette had tried to scare her with that ghost business. She had a sudden suspicion about how Margaret found her way into the bedroom. The note was a nice touch.

"I'll spread a blanket on the rug," said Bonnie.

"There are perfectly good beds upstairs," said Aunt Nell.

"My ankle hurts," Bonnie said.

"My leg hurts *and* my head hurts."

Bonnie sighed.

"There's some aspirin in the cabinet by the kitchen sink and you could make yourself an ice pack. That would maybe help a little. Go on now and get some rest," Aunt Nell spoke more gently.

Bonnie stood up, tucking Margaret under her arm. The pain had lessened. Only her ankle hurt now. "Which way is the kitchen?" she asked.

Aunt Nell pointed down a hallway off of her room.

Bonnie limped out of the room.

A night-light was burning near the sink. Bonnie found the aspirin and shook two of the white pills into her hand. She put them in her mouth and washed them down with water caught in her cupped hands. She decided not to bother with the ice.

Rather than disturb Aunt Nell again, Bonnie circled through the dining room and living room to the main hallway.

Using the railing, she hopped up the stairs on her left foot. She didn't find the note in the hallway or on the stairway.

Bonnie paused before the door to Lynette's room. She knocked softly. When no one answered, Bonnie pushed the door open. Lynette was curled up on top of the covers, breathing evenly. She didn't stir in the slightest.

In her own room, Bonnie sat on the side of her bed, dangling Margaret between her knees. It gave her the strangest feeling to look into a doll's face so much like her own.

She felt around on the bed for the note. The red printing should show up easily against the white sheets. She looked on the bedside table, then on the floor. The note was nowhere to be found. Had she imagined it? Bonnie wondered. Probably she'd dropped it in the hallway and it had drifted into a dark corner. Tomorrow, first thing, she'd find the note and take it to her aunt. For some reason, someone was trying to scare her. And doing a good job of it.

Bonnie placed the doll on the pillow and tucked the sheet around her. She lay down beside the doll, then reached toward the lamp to turn it off.

"Let's leave it on, okay Margaret?" she said to the doll.

Bonnie turned on her side and faced Margaret. She pulled the doll a little closer.

Her ankle throbbed. Bonnie sat up and felt it with her fingertips. There didn't seem to be any bones sticking out and she could move it.

Bonnie nestled Margaret in the crook of her arm and felt a little less alone.

# 5

Bonnie awoke, still holding onto the Margaret doll. She dressed quickly, and slipped as quietly as she could into the hallway. Bonnie carefully searched the stairs for the note Margaret had delivered the night before. She couldn't even find any dust, much less a scrap of paper. Her aunts certainly kept a clean house.

Bonnie proceeded down the stairs and into the kitchen. Her ankle, although still sore, felt much better. Her main complaint was hunger. *As usual*, she thought. Bonnie propped Margaret on the kitchen counter and opened the refrigerator door.

"Bonnie? Is that you?" Aunt Nell called out from her studio.

"It's me," Bonnie answered.

"We have breakfast in here," her aunt said.

Bonnie had hoped everyone else was still in bed. She wanted a chance to look around on her own.

She picked Margaret up, took a deep breath, and headed down the back hallway to her aunt's studio.

Aunt Nell was not alone. Lynette and Aunt Mollie were with her.

Bonnie tried not to limp as she entered the studio. After all, Aunt Nell had a broken leg and she hardly mentioned it.

Someone had pulled a table up to Aunt Nell's bed. A pitcher filled with iced orange juice sat in the middle of the table surrounded by plates piled high with doughnuts and rolls.

"Here, darlin', you sit down right here." Aunt Mollie pulled a chair up to the table and sat Bonnie down.

Lynette was sitting on the edge of Aunt Nell's bed dressed in an outfit identical to the one she had had on the day before except that the T-shirt she now wore was red.

Aunt Nell was busily writing something on a clipboard and didn't even look up.

"Did you sleep well?" Aunt Mollie asked. Without waiting for an answer, she proceeded, "I got up this morning and thought, 'What would Bonnie want for breakfast? I'll bet she would like homemade cinnamon rolls,' I said to myself. 'No, she'd probably like doughnuts,' I said on second thought. Then, I thought rolls again, then doughnuts, so I made both!"

"Thanks, Aunt Mollie. I do like them both," Bonnie said, taking one of each.

"Dad told me all about your doughnuts," Bonnie continued. "It was his suggestion to get the recipe that gave me the idea for my family history project. I want to do a book of family recipes."

Aunt Mollie beamed. She placed a second doughnut on Bonnie's plate.

"A recipe book!" Aunt Nell's voice was tinged with disbelief.

"That's what she said," said Aunt Mollie.

"No, no, no! I thought the dolls were going to be your project," insisted Aunt Nell.

"I've got recipes going back as far as the dolls," said Aunt Mollie.

Bonnie took a bite of her roll. Visiting with her aunts and listening to their constant bickering during meals might be just what she needed to help her lose weight. It certainly made her lose her appetite.

"As soon as you know a little more about our dolls, you'll forget all about that silly recipe idea," Aunt Nell said to Bonnie.

"I'll start going through my recipes today," said Aunt Mollie as she glared at her sister.

"Bonnie," Aunt Nell looked at her over the clipboard, "and Lynette, I want you girls to go over to the museum and clean up any mess we left yesterday. The boxes I have stored down there also need to be sorted through. I'd really hoped to be able to do that myself."

"That's not a two-person job," said Lynette. "I can do it by myself. Bonnie can stay up here with you."

"Thank you, Lynette. But I'd like Bonnie to get some experience with the dolls. There's so much down there, I don't really know where to tell you to begin. Don't worry about anything not related to the dolls. We can move all that over here to the attic. I especially want you to look for old tools. I need some for a display I have planned on the doll-making process."

"Really, I think I can handle it. Bonnie can stay here and help you decide what dolls to take over," Lynette suggested.

"I want her to go to the museum," Aunt Nell said firmly.

Bonnie watched and listened to the exchange, feeling uncomfortable.

"Bonnie, darlin'! Where'd you get this doll?" Aunt Mollie pulled Margaret off of Bonnie's lap and held her over the table.

Bonnie heard Lynette gasp.

"Evidently Margaret had been taking a little vacation from it all under the bed in Bonnie's room," Aunt Nell answered for her.

"Looks like that vacation did her a world of good," Aunt Mollie said.

"I found her under my bed and . . ." Bonnie started to explain.

"Didn't you clean that room before she arrived?" Aunt Nell asked Aunt Mollie.

"Of course I did! I sweep that room once a week whether someone is visiting or not," said Aunt Mollie.

"Why didn't you find the doll then?"

"Someone brought the doll in last night, with a note," Bonnie said. She looked at Lynette.

Lynette started to gather up dirty glasses and plates.

"A note," said Aunt Mollie.

"It said — " Bonnie started again, only to be interrupted again.

"And where is the note?" asked Aunt Nell.

"I think I dropped it last night when I came down here to show you the doll. It must have gotten under something. I can't find it," Bonnie admitted, feeling a little embarrassed.

Aunt Nell looked at Bonnie over the top of her glasses.

"I swept the stairs and hallway already this morning and I don't remember seeing any note," said Aunt Mollie.

Bonnie decided not to say anything else about the note for now. Maybe it would turn up later.

"I just realized how much you resemble Margaret, Bonnie. It's amazing," said Aunt Mollie.

Bonnie picked up the dirty dishes Lynette couldn't carry.

"You girls need to eat more doughnuts, more rolls. You're both a couple of sticks," said Aunt Mollie, holding the plate out to them.

"Not right now," Bonnie said.

Lynette shook her head. She started into the kitchen.

Bonnie followed.

"I'll do those dishes," Aunt Mollie's voice thundered after them. "Go on up and find that stuff for Nell before she has a conniption fit."

"Bonnie," Aunt Nell called out. "I'm going to keep Margaret with me to make sure she doesn't go on any more *vacations.*"

Bonnie was disappointed. She wanted to keep Margaret in her room.

"It's going to be hot today," said Lynette.

To Bonnie there was no "going to be" about it. It was already hot. She pulled her T-shirt away from where it was sticking to her skin to show Lynette she wasn't telling her anything new.

"Then we'd better get going before it gets any hotter," said Bonnie. "You lead the way."

Bonnie followed Lynette out the back door and across the small field she'd run across so quickly the day before. She didn't plan to do much running today. Her ankle was too sore.

When they reached the museum, Lynette took the key out of her pocket. She turned it first one way, then the other.

"Darn this lock. It's so contrary," said Lynette. She let go of the key and flexed her fingers.

Bonnie heard the honk of a car horn coming from the direction of the gravel road running beside the museum.

She looked around to see who it was. The car was the same car that had stopped in front of Aunt Mollie's restaurant the day before. She quickly looked away.

The car horn honked again, this time playing an off-key rendition of "Dixie."

"Hey, girls! Why don't you come for a ride with us?" one of the boys called out in a high-pitched voice.

"Jerks," Lynette said under her breath. She fiddled with the key again.

"Who are they? I saw them yesterday, at Aunt Mollie's restaurant," Bonnie said.

"What an impressive welcoming committee they must have been. Just ignore them. They're nothing but a couple of troublemakers," said Lynette.

The horn sounded again. Bonnie refused to turn around.

The lock finally clicked and the door swung open.

"It wouldn't surprise me a bit if they didn't make all the mess down here," Lynette added. "Unless it was . . ." She didn't finish.

Bonnie was only half-listening to what Lynette said as she took her first good look at the museum's interior.

The walls were white plaster, the floor covered in a tile meant to look like brick. There was one large window on each side of the room and an arched doorway leading into a smaller back room. The main room was large and bright. Shelves and display cases were scattered about waiting to be installed. A big desk took up one corner. The table was exactly as it had been yesterday — on its side surrounded by dolls. Boxes and trunks covered much of the remaining floor space.

The smaller back room was dominated by a stone fireplace flanked by cupboards.

"Your aunt usually works up at the house so this building has been used for storage for years. You should have seen it before we cleaned it up," said Lynette.

"Is this it? Just the two rooms?" asked Bonnie.

"Mrs. Boone plans to build an office on to the back once the museum gets going. And maybe a snack bar if Mrs. Snyder ever agrees. But for now, yeah, this is it."

Bonnie continued to stare at the boxes, trunks,

and odds and ends piled before her. "What are we looking for?" she asked.

"If you find any tools, show them to me. I think I know what Mrs. Boone needs for her exhibit. And set aside any doll stuff. Otherwise, just keep track of what is in each box," Lynette said. "Why don't you start going through those boxes and trunks under the window?"

"Did you happen to notice whether that Margaret doll was in my room last night when we first went in?" Bonnie asked.

"Mrs. Boone said you found the doll under your bed," said Lynette.

"I hit the table with my backpack and the doll fell off it."

"You just must not have seen it earlier."

Bonnie took a deep breath, trying to keep herself from getting angry. "You don't think I wouldn't notice a doll that looked just like me? Did *you* see it?"

Lynette shook her head.

"And there was a note, too. It was a warning note. I think somebody came into my room when I was out on the porch and left that Margaret doll on the table beside my bed. I just can't figure out who or why. Was someone just trying to scare me?" Bonnie watched Lynette carefully for a response.

"I didn't do it, if that's what you're wondering," Lynette said, not even bothering to look up at Bonnie.

Bonnie didn't bother to acknowledge her denial.

"It *had* to be there all the time," Lynette said.

Bonnie couldn't figure out why no one else seemed to think it was strange at all to have a doll that looked just like you appear magically in your room holding a warning.

She decided to let it go for now. Maybe Aunt Mollie knew something about the doll, although she had seemed surprised to see it that morning. Aunt Nell was probably right. Bonnie had been tired and feeling a little nervous about the whole situation. She was probably making a big deal out of nothing. Maybe the doll was under the bed the whole time and the note was something that just happened to get stuck to the doll. Maybe neither had anything at all to do with her.

Bonnie leaned down to pick up the dolls scattered all over the floor. When she'd piled them all neatly beside the overturned table, she carefully threaded her way across the floor to the window.

She opened a trunk. It was full of soft doll bodies — no heads — carefully stacked like wood. She slammed the lid shut.

"I don't see any evidence of the stuff you guys were talking about last night. You know, the fire, the paint, the broken windows," said Bonnie.

"Everything's been fixed. The fire was in the fireplace. It just caused smoke damage because the chimney was stopped up. The windows are all new. The paint job is new. The floor is new."

"And you think those boys might have done it?" said Bonnie.

"Maybe," said Lynette.

"Who else could it be?" asked Bonnie. "And what about the police? Aren't they doing anything about it?"

"They drive by from time to time and say they're trying to keep an eye on things a little more. But as far as *who*, it could be someone who doesn't want the museum here in Callaway," said Lynette.

"Who would care? I mean, what is there to object to in a doll museum?"

Lynette answered slowly. "What if someone wanted another kind of museum here?" she said. "Callaway isn't big enough for two museums."

"Who?" asked Bonnie.

"Or maybe it was someone who broke in thinking they'd find something valuable and when they didn't, they trashed the place," said Lynette.

"That sounds like those two guys," said Bonnie.

"But three times? I'd think they would have learned there's nothing here after one try. And who else wanted a museum here?"

"Think about it," said Lynette.

"Think about what?" Bonnie didn't know where to begin. She only knew six people in the entire town and she was willing to bet it was the tough-looking guys in the loud car who were responsible for the trouble. She planned to keep her eyes open for those two.

"How long have you known my aunts?" asked Bonnie, changing the subject.

"As long as I can remember," Lynette said. "Grandma always watched me while Mama worked even though Grandma worked, too. Mrs. Boone didn't mind if I came along. See, she helped your aunt in the doll business.

"Grandma is one of the reasons I want to find those missing dolls. She told me over and over how *our* family was just as important to the doll making as yours was. Hmph!" She slammed a lid shut on a box.

"It's probably true," said Bonnie.

"It *is* true. And as soon as I get some proof . . ."

Bonnie looked around the room at the boxes stacked everywhere. "Lynette, is there any chance your family's dolls might be in one of these boxes?" she asked. She continued to the next box while waiting for the girl to answer.

"I guess it's possible, but somehow I don't think they're in such an obvious place or someone would have found them by now."

"How could anyone find anything in all this?" said Bonnie, still seeing nothing that resembled the tools her aunt had described.

"Mrs. Boone has a vague idea of what's here," said Lynette.

"Omigosh! Look at these hats!" Bonnie pulled a large hat out of a trunk. It was trimmed with ragged feathers. She plopped it on her head. "Is there a mirror anywhere?"

"Over there," Lynette said.

Bonnie made her way to the mirror holding the hat in place. The glass was so covered with dust, she could hardly see her reflection. She pulled a rag out of a box sitting on the floor and wiped a circle clean.

"I love old clothes like these and there are just trunks full of them," Bonnie said excitedly.

Behind her, Bonnie could see Lynette's reflection in the mirror watching. "Go pick out a hat for yourself and bring it over here," she urged.

Lynette looked toward the trunk full of hats. She finally crawled over a stack of boxes and started going through it.

"Bring another one for me, too," said Bonnie.

Lynette joined her at the mirror carrying two hats, a straw hat and one fashioned from felt.

"Let me clean some more of the mirror so you can see yourself," said Bonnie, picking out another rag.

Lynette grabbed Bonnie's wrist. "Where'd you get that?" she asked, taking the rag out of Bonnie's hand and smoothing it carefully on the floor.

"There's a whole box of them here," said Bonnie, puzzled.

"Look at it! Look! Don't you know what it is?"

"Oh, no! Is that what Aunt Nell wanted for her display?" Bonnie looked at the dusty, wadded up pieces of cloth with dismay.

"No! They're doll clothes!"

Bonnie examined them more closely. "They are! Do you think I could wash them? Are they ruined? I didn't know."

"Bonnie! Don't they look like the same kind of clothes the black doll was wearing in the picture in the book?"

"They do!" Bonnie took the remaining dresses out of the box and lined them up beside the one Lynette had rescued.

"Maybe the dolls *are* here," Bonnie said, looking around.

Lynette shook her head. "I really don't think so, but I've never noticed these dresses before either."

She looked thoughtful. "Maybe, if we show them to her, your aunt will believe me — believe that there were more black dolls."

"I'd really like to find those dolls," Bonnie said.

"I'm sure you would. That would be one more exhibit to pack into the museum," Lynette said sharply. She threw the hat down on the floor and stalked away.

"Lynette," Bonnie said. "I don't want them for me. I want them for you."

"Well, I guess Mrs. Boone and Mrs. Snyder would be the ones to say who they belonged to anyway," said Lynette. She picked up the hat, dusted it off, and carefully replaced it in the trunk.

"Aunt Nell may want them in the museum, but Aunt Mollie probably doesn't care about them at all since they aren't edible," Bonnie said.

Lynette laughed. "You're not at all like I thought you'd be."

"What do you mean by that?"

"I mean you're from the city, working on a project for some special class for smart kids, and all this will be yours someday. Yet you don't seem one bit possessive about it." Lynette pointed around the room.

"I don't feel a bit possessive. I don't even like dolls that much," Bonnie confessed. "I'm lots more interested in collecting recipes that have been handed down. My project is supposed to be a cookbook. Aunt Nell doesn't seem to understand."

"She doesn't see much beyond the dolls. That's one reason she has so much trouble with Mrs. Snyder. She doesn't give your aunt Mollie any credit for having cooking talent."

"Then Aunt Nell's not going to like me much either. All my talents are in the kitchen, too." Bonnie patted her stomach.

"I'll help you get your recipes if you'll help me talk to Mrs. Boone about the black dolls," said Lynette.

"Deal," said Bonnie.

A smile spread over Lynette's face.

Bonnie smiled, too.

"But we'd better find that stuff for your aunt first," Lynette said. "Of course, it won't hurt to look for the dolls at the same time."

"Bonnie! Lynette!" It was Aunt Mollie, sweat streaming down her red face, looking in the window. "Nell wants you girls to come home and give her a progress report."

"Darn! Just when we were getting started," grumbled Bonnie.

"We'd better go," said Lynette.

Bonnie brushed off her clothes, arms, and legs. "I feel so yucky!"

"Me, too."

"Don't forget to take the doll clothes to show to Aunt Nell," said Bonnie.

"You said *you'd* try to talk to her," said Lynette. "She doesn't even hear me when I bring up that subject anymore."

"Girls! Are you coming?" Aunt Mollie yelled from outside.

Bonnie scooped up a few of the doll dresses and limped as fast as she could up the hill to the house.

# 6

"Aunt Nell, look at what we found!" Bonnie held out the doll clothes.

"Goodness, child, what are these?" Aunt Nell picked up one of the dresses by a sleeve and frowned at it.

"They're doll clothes. We think they were probably made for black dolls." Bonnie saw her aunt look at Lynette. "They're almost exactly like the picture in the book. Darn! I wish I had that book. I'll be right back."

Bonnie turned to go get the book and found Marc blocking her way.

"Hi, remember me from the bus station?" he asked.

Bonnie quickly smoothed her hair and straightened her clothes. "Yes, of course, hi, Marc," she spoke rapidly. "In fact, I'm going up to get that book you left me."

She started off again.

"What book?" Aunt Nell demanded.

"A book on the history of Callaway," said Bonnie.

"Yankee hogwash!" Aunt Nell burst out.

Marc quickly covered up a chuckle.

"Aunt Nell — " Bonnie began.

"That book is biased. Don't you laugh, young man." She shook her finger at Marc. "Your grandfather totally ignored the fact that most of the residents of Callaway fought under the Confederate flag and were slaveowners. He didn't even mention the fact that Callaway seceded from the Union!"

"Mrs. Boone, there's an entire chapter covering rebel activity during the Civil War," Marc said.

"And one on the Yankees and one on, of all things, the Underground Railroad!" said an indignant Aunt Nell.

"But not a single chapter on slaves," Bonnie heard Lynette say under her breath.

"No wonder about that though. The Allens were no doubt right in the middle of that movement," Aunt Nell continued.

"Maybe, maybe not. That's one of the things that makes it so interesting," said Marc, "not knowing who, how, or where exactly the Railroad operated. If my grandfather ever locates the tunnels . . ."

"Is he still looking for those, that old fool," said

Aunt Nell, shaking her head. "Bonnie, don't bother getting that book. I know exactly what you're talking about.

"These are patterns that were used to fit the clothes on the dolls before more expensive fabric was cut into. I do that myself, only I use muslin." She tossed the dresses aside.

"Did you find the stuff I asked you to find?"

Lynette gathered the dresses into a neat pile.

"No, ma'am," Bonnie answered.

"It's taking too long. Move all those boxes of junk outside. Marc, you can help. I'll send someone down with a truck to carry it all back here to the attic," said Aunt Nell.

Bonnie felt a stab of disappointment. She wanted to look for Lynette's dolls.

"How about we take a picnic to the creek and cool off a little first?" Marc asked Aunt Nell.

"A picnic! You children aren't going to get a thing done as long as I'm tied to this bed."

"I promise we won't stay long and we'll work twice as hard when we get to the museum," said Marc.

"Let 'em go, Nell." Aunt Mollie joined them, fanning her face with a large straw hat. "It's murderous hot today. I'll even pack up the lunch."

Aunt Mollie dropped her hat and a large straw bag with rolls of paper sticking out of it right where she stood. As she walked toward the kitchen, some of the papers fell out of the bag and rolled along behind Aunt Mollie.

Bonnie leaned down to catch the rolls.

Aunt Mollie caught them first.

"Grave rubbings," she said. "Such a fascinating place, that cemetery."

Bonnie stood up quickly, not wanting to even touch the paper.

"I'll be right back with that picnic," Aunt Mollie promised.

The walk to the creek caused Bonnie's ankle to throb. The first thing she did when they reached the clearing was kick off her shoe and stick her foot in the cold, rushing water.

Lynette handed Bonnie a sandwich.

"It's beautiful here," Bonnie said. "And so much cooler."

"What's wrong with your foot?" Marc asked.

"I fell down the steps last night and twisted it. It's sore, but Aunt Nell says it will be all right."

"Maybe my grandfather should look at it."

"I'll be okay," Bonnie said. "Marc, when did your grandfather write that history you gave me?"

"Several years ago," he answered. "And Grandfather almost started the Civil War again, at least as far as your aunt was concerned."

"Why?"

"Mrs. Boone thinks he didn't give enough attention to the southerners who she claims built up this area. This little feud goes way back to the Civil War. Your family sympathized with the South and owned slaves. While the Allens fought for the North and were abolitionists, completely opposed to slavery."

"Yankees," Bonnie said, trying to imitate Aunt Nell.

"You bet. Colonel Scott accused our family of helping slaves from around here escape on the Underground Railroad, but Grandfather hasn't been able to prove or disprove it. There are supposed to be tunnels and hidey-holes all over the place, but no one knows where," Marc explained.

"Yet," a man's voice filled the clearing. "But I intend to find out."

Bonnie jerked her foot out of the water and jumped up, almost falling into the creek, the pain hit her so hard.

"What's wrong here?" The tall, white-haired man caught Bonnie's arm, then leaned down to examine her ankle.

"This is my grandfather," Marc informed the startled Bonnie before she pulled away.

"It's swollen and must be very sore," Dr. Allen said as he gently probed the tender ankle, "but it's sprained, not broken. Wrapping it in an elastic bandage will help and so will ice and staying off of it. Marc, who is my newest patient?"

"This is Bonnie. She's Mrs. Boone's niece."

"Glad to meet you, Bonnie." Dr. Allen shook her hand. "I'll send a bandage over with Marc. He'll show you how to wrap it. You don't happen to have an elastic bandage in one of those pockets of yours, do you?" Dr. Allen asked his grandson.

Marc stuck his hand in his pocket and pulled out a fistful of assorted junk. He held it out to his grandfather.

Dr. Allen and Lynette laughed.

Bonnie wasn't sure why.

"I carry a lot of stuff with me in case I need it," Marc explained to Bonnie as he stuffed everything back in his pocket. "It's gotten to be kind of a joke."

"I keep telling him he ought to carry a purse," said Dr. Allen. He turned to Lynette. "How are things at the museum?" he asked.

"Getting there," Lynette responded.

"Tell Mrs. Boone I'd be glad to help her out some if she's willing to take help from an old Yankee," Dr. Allen said, his eyes twinkling.

"I'll tell her," said Bonnie.

"Mrs. Boone already told her all about you," Marc informed his grandfather.

"Is that right?" Dr. Allen smiled at Bonnie. "I just ran into your Aunt Mollie in the cemetery.

She doesn't seem to share Nell's strong dislike of Yankees."

*Why do these people spend so much time in the cemetery?* Bonnie wondered.

"We really need to get to the museum," Lynette reminded them. "We haven't gotten much done today, and Mrs. Boone would rest a lot better if she thought we were working."

"You kids run along. I think I'll stay here where it's cool for a while," said Dr. Allen. "Nice to meet you, Bonnie. Come see me if that ankle doesn't get better."

"Thanks again, Dr. Allen," said Bonnie.

"Anything left of that lunch?" the doctor asked.

Marc reached in, pulled out a doughnut, and handed it to his grandfather.

"One of Mollie's doughnuts. Ambrosia!" he said. Dr. Allen sat down on a tree stump beside the stream.

"I'm going to help out at the museum," Marc said to his grandfather.

"It's awfully hot today. Don't work too hard," said Dr. Allen.

"Don't let Mrs. Boone hear you giving us advice like that," Lynette said with a laugh.

"It'll be our secret." Dr. Allen waved as the girls followed Marc.

"We can cut through here." Marc pointed through the trees. "It'll be shorter."

"I don't know," Lynette said, looking at Bonnie.

"C'mon." Marc started off.

"Where are we going?" Bonnie whispered to Lynette as she tried to keep from getting tangled in the branches.

Before Lynette could answer, they broke through the trees.

I should have known, Bonnie thought, as she found herself standing in the cemetery.

# 7

Bonnie's eyes traveled from tombstone to tombstone. There were flat stones, rectangular stones, curved stones, but the most compelling were the intricately designed gravestones with everything from a smooth round ball to an angel to a horse sitting atop them.

She took a second look at the horse. It was the one in the picture on the cover of Dr. Allen's book.

It was another monument, however, that really captured Bonnie's attention. Close to the front of the graveyard, a tall, gray dome loomed, making all of the headstones look small, almost insignificant.

Bonnie had a definite feeling that the marker would have the name SCOTT carved on it.

"What's the holdup?" Marc called over his shoulder.

"Just looking around," Bonnie answered.

Marc was almost through the cemetery.

Lynette, Bonnie noticed gratefully, had stayed close by her.

Marc came running back. "We aren't going to get anything done if you guys keep poking along, and what's Mrs. Boone going to have to say about that?"

Suddenly Bonnie stopped entirely. "What's that dome-shaped building over there?" she asked.

Marc and Lynette looked at one another and grinned.

"That's the Scott family mausoleum," Marc answered.

"Mausoleum!" Bonnie exclaimed.

Marc nodded, still grinning. "Your ancesters are enshrined forever in the base of that monument. There's even a door so you can go inside and pay your respects."

Bonnie shuddered.

"You can't see anything but bronze plaques with the names on them," Lynette added.

"And there isn't any more room. The rest of you Scotts will have to be planted in the ground like everybody else," Marc said.

Bonnie stared at the tomb, fascinated. She couldn't decide whether she wanted to go inside in the worst way or whether she would never, ever under any circumstances go inside.

"Let's go." Marc grabbed Bonnie's hand and

pulled her along. "It would have taken us less time to walk all the way around."

They approached the museum from the rear.

Marc tried to open the door.

"It's locked," said Lynette, handing him the key.

Bonnie followed Marc inside the museum. She realized they still needed to clean the spots of blood off the floor.

Lynette immediately began to scoot boxes nearer the door.

Marc squatted down and inspected the table.

"Can you fix it?" asked Bonnie.

Marc frowned. "Look at this," he said. He pointed to one of the supports that held the leg in place.

Bonnie leaned down and looked at it. The break was completely smooth, almost like it had been sawed through.

Lynette joined them. "What? Can you fix it?"

"I may be able to fix it, but it looks to me like someone deliberately cut it so this table would collapse."

Lynette drew away. "No," she said firmly. "It's an old table. It just snapped when Mrs. Boone climbed up there."

"Lynette, the break is too smooth. Someone deliberately sabotaged the table," Bonnie said.

"No one would want to hurt Mrs. Boone," said Lynette.

"I doubt whoever did this thought she would actually climb up on the table," Marc said.

"That's just too mean," Lynette said, almost to herself.

Bonnie tried to pick up one of the boxes and carry it to the door. It made her ankle hurt even worse. She went into the back room to wet a rag to use to wipe up the blood.

As Bonnie turned the water off, she heard something. It sounded like a cat.

"Come here a minute," she called out to Marc and Lynette.

They came to the doorway.

"Do you hear a cat?" Bonnie asked, still listening carefully.

Marc and Lynette stood quietly.

*Meow.*

Bonnie went to the door and looked outside. No cat appeared.

*Meooow.*

"It sounds like it's *inside*," said Marc.

Bonnie searched the room, pulling back flaps on all the boxes she could reach.

*Meow, meow, meow.*

She found no sign of a cat.

Bonnie walked slowly around the edge of the room, listening carefully.

*Mew, mew, meow*, she heard.

"Sounds like a kitten," Marc said.

"Shh!" Bonnie put a finger to her lips.

*Meow.*

"It's coming from over here, behind this wall," Bonnie said, pointing to the very back of the room.

"No," said Marc.

"Listen."

*Meow, meow, meow, meow*. The cat was sounding more frantic.

Bonnie stopped beside the cupboard built into the wall beside the fireplace. She leaned her ear against the cupboard door.

*Meow, meow, mew, mew, mew*, she heard the cat cry.

"It's in here!"

Bonnie pulled the door open. Nothing.

*Meowowowowow!* she heard.

Bonnie stepped inside and pressed her ear against the back wall.

The wall moved.

# 8

Bonnie let out a short scream and pulled back before she tumbled into the void before her. The wall swung back into place.

Marc and Lynette crowded inside the small cupboard.

"Don't! Move back!" said Bonnie.

"What's wrong?" Marc asked.

"The wall — it moved!"

Marc and Lynette stepped back.

"That's ridiculous," said Marc.

Bonnie pushed the back of the cupboard with her hand. Slowly, the wall rotated, leaving a black opening where the wall had once been.

Bonnie put her hand through the opening and felt nothing. She sank to her knees and looked over the edge.

"The cat's down in this hole," Bonnie said unnecessarily. The volume of the meowing had increased substantially.

She leaned over the hole again. "There's a ladder here. Is there a flashlight around?"

A light appeared over Bonnie's shoulder, aimed down into the opening. She reached up and took the flashlight, playing the beam around the hole.

"I can't see anything from here. I'm going down," Bonnie said.

"I'm coming, too," Marc said.

"No," Lynette objected.

"Why not? It's probably a cellar or something. Someone has to get the cat."

"There's no cellar," Lynette said, "just a crawl space. Your aunt has said she wished they'd thought to put in a cellar so we'd have more storage down here."

"Now she'll have some storage," Bonnie said.

"You guys, I think we should tell Mrs. Boone or Mrs. Snyder about it before we go down there," Lynette said.

"We'll tell them, but we need to know what this room is first. You don't have to come down," said Bonnie.

"If you're both going, I will too," Lynette said reluctantly.

Bonnie clambered down the ladder and started shining the light around the small space. Marc joined her, then Lynette.

"It's nothing," Bonnie said, feeling disappointed, "just an empty hole."

"Not completely empty." Marc picked up a tiny, orange kitten huddled in a corner, shaking with fright."

"It's so sweet." Bonnie took the cat from Marc. "Now how in the world did it get down here?"

"Someone must know this room is here. And they must have been here recently, because the cat got inside," said Lynette.

"Hello-o-o! Anybody here?"

Bonnie heard a voice upstairs.

"Quick! Up!" she said.

Lynette went first, then Bonnie with the kitten clinging to her shirt.

"Anybody here?" the voice asked again.

"Not a word of this to anyone else until I tell Aunt Nell," Bonnie made them promise.

Lynette hurried to the door to let a man in.

"I'm supposed to haul some boxes from here up to the house," Bonnie heard him tell Lynette.

Bonnie handed the kitten to Marc. She closed the revolving wall and slammed the cupboard door shut before the man came inside.

"I want to go talk to Aunt Nell," she said in a hushed voice to Marc and Lynette as the man busied himself carrying boxes outside and loading them on a truck.

"Go ahead. We'll stay here and help him with this stuff," said Marc.

"What about the kitten?" asked Lynette.

"Can I take it up to the house?" Bonnie asked, not sure how her aunts felt about cats.

"Why don't we leave it here for now? You'd better ask first. We'll get it some milk and water and let it stay inside the museum and be a watch cat," Marc suggested.

"Some watch cat," Bonnie said. "It's so tiny. Shouldn't we try to find out who it belongs to?"

"Somebody probably dumped it out alongside the road. It happens out here all the time. People think that's a way to get rid of an animal they don't want anymore," said Lynette.

"Then this little guy is lucky we found him," said Bonnie, petting the cat one last time.

"You go on and tell Mrs. Boone about the room. We'll catch up with you later," Marc said.

"I hate to leave all this mess for you guys," Bonnie said.

"Just go. There'll still be plenty for you to do when you get back," said Lynette.

Bonnie took off across the field to her aunts'. In the excitement of finding the room, she'd forgotten about her ankle, and now the throbbing seemed even worse.

Bonnie could see Aunt Mollie standing outside on the porch.

"Aunt Mollie!" she called out, waving her hand to make sure her aunt saw her.

Aunt Mollie walked over to the steps and stood there, crossing her arms over her chest.

Bonnie reached the porch.

Her aunt was looking at her with no sign of a smile on her face.

"What's the matter?" Bonnie asked, fear replacing the excitement in her stomach.

"I want you to go straight to your room and get in bed, young lady," Aunt Mollie said sternly. "Dr. Allen just called me and told me all about this ankle. I was on my way over to the museum to carry you home when I saw you limping your way over here."

"It's fine," Bonnie protested. "I need to talk to Aunt Nell."

"Nell needs some rest. That leg is really painin' her. You're going to rest, too. We're going to have to get a hospital license here if you gals don't straighten up."

Aunt Mollie took Bonnie by the arm and guided her up to her room.

"But Aunt Mollie, over at the museum . . ."

"The museum will still be there when you get up." Aunt Mollie pointed at the bed.

Bonnie sat down on the edge of it.

"Lie down," her aunt ordered.

Bonnie did.

Aunt Mollie fluffed pillows and stuck one under Bonnie's ankle. She pulled the shades down and turned on a small fan sitting on the dresser.

"You rest. When you get up, I'll have a nice snack waiting."

Aunt Mollie pulled the door closed behind her.

# 9

"Bonnie! Bonnie!" someone was whispering from behind a tombstone.

Bonnie reached out to slap away the hand that was holding her shoulder so she couldn't get away. She had to get out of the cemetery, but the tombstones stretched on and on and her ankle hurt.

"Bonnie!"

Bonnie awoke and saw Lynette standing beside her bed. She sat up, shaking her head and trying to think where she really was, glad to be out of the cemetery, out of her nightmare.

"I thought you weren't going to wake up," said Lynette.

Bonnie lay back down and looked at Lynette perched on the side of her bed. "I was having a bad dream," she explained hoarsely.

"What did your aunt say about the room?" Lynette asked.

"I didn't get to tell her. Aunt Mollie wouldn't

let me in to talk to her. In fact, she made me come up here and take a nap — like a three-year-old. When I tried to tell her about the room, she wouldn't listen. How long have I been asleep?"

"Pretty long. I was starting to worry that something had happened when you didn't come back down to the museum." Lynette smiled. "I came to check and Mrs. Snyder wouldn't even let me come upstairs. She still won't let anyone in to see Mrs. Boone. I finally convinced her that you'd slept long enough. She's really getting into this nursing."

"I meant to lie down for just a minute. I guess I was more tired than I thought. I didn't sleep very well last night," said Bonnie. "Aunt Mollie wouldn't let you talk to Aunt Nell either? That's kind of strange. I can't imagine that Aunt Nell doesn't want to talk to us. She's so worried we aren't doing anything. By the way, did you finish at the museum?"

"Finish? We must have carried over a hundred boxes. There are more than it looks. We loaded the truck twice and still didn't get everything moved out of the museum. Marc did fix the table, however."

Bonnie rubbed her eyes, sat up, and stretched. "What time is it?"

"About six-thirty."

"Six-thirty! I've been asleep for almost three

hours." Bonnie swung her legs over the side of the bed. "I'll never get to sleep tonight."

"Maybe that'll be a good thing," Lynette said.

Bonnie was at the mirror rebraiding her hair. She turned to Lynette. "What do you mean?"

"Someone was at the museum while we were gone to lunch," Lynette said. "That box of doll clothes, the dresses we thought might belong to those missing dolls, I couldn't find them when we were loading things on the truck."

"Maybe you just forgot where you put it."

Lynette shook her head. "We checked *everything* and I can't find the box of doll clothes. And this time I'm sure we locked the door. I remember Marc unlocking it when we came back."

"Unless whoever let the cat inside unlocked it and locked it again. Or locked it because we forgot."

"It's not Mrs. Boone. She couldn't even get down to the museum, much less down in that room," said Lynette.

"Maybe the box of clothes didn't disappear from the museum. It could have been taken off the truck after everything was loaded," Bonnie suggested.

"Well those clothes are going to be the last thing anyone takes. I'm spending the night down there tonight," said Lynette.

"Aunt Nell won't let you," said Bonnie.

"She won't know."

"Then I'm coming with you."

"I was hoping you'd say that," Lynette said. "Not only will we keep someone from getting in and doing further damage, but maybe we'll find out once and for all who is doing it. The telephone man came after you left, so we even have a phone to call the police."

"Can we eat something first?" asked Bonnie.

"Mrs. Snyder has dinner all fixed. It's in the refrigerator, a salad, ham, a pie, and who knows what else. I've already had mine. I think I'll go on to the museum," said Lynette.

"I'll hurry. But what should I tell my aunts?"

"Mrs. Boone is asleep and Mrs. Snyder isn't around. Just leave them a note and say we're at Marc's," said Lynette. "I want to tell them about the secret room face-to-face. We'll come back up here after a while. You'll hurry?"

"I'll hurry," Bonnie promised.

The two girls went downstairs together.

"How's your ankle?" Lynette asked.

"Better. Do you know if Marc left that bandage like his grandfather told him to?"

"I don't think so, but he said he'd be over later," said Lynette. She paused, her hand on the doorknob.

"What's wrong?" asked Bonnie.

"Marc's grandfather wanted to start a museum, too, an historical museum. Your aunt just got hers going first," said Lynette.

"So?"

"I'm just trying to figure out who keeps messing with Mrs. Boone's museum."

"You don't think Dr. Allen . . . he's so nice," said Bonnie.

"He came right through the cemetery from the direction of the museum about the time the box disappeared," said Lynette.

"I thought you thought it was those guys, the ones who drove by and honked this morning."

"It *could* be them. But taking the time to cut a table leg so it would collapse? That's not really their style. And why would they want a box of old doll clothes?"

"Maybe they didn't have time to look to see what was inside the box and they wanted to take *something*. Do you really think Dr. Allen would want to hurt someone? And why would *he* want the doll clothes? To tell you the truth, they looked like rags to me," Bonnie said.

Lynette chewed on her lower lip. "It could be someone else entirely. Someone just waiting for the dolls to get down to the museum then — " she snapped her fingers, " — they'll be gone, stolen, no more museum."

"Aunt Nell would die."

"I know. That's why we have to make sure we catch whoever it is who's doing these things." Lynette opened the door. She turned around one last time. "Then we can concentrate on finding my dolls."

Bonnie peeked in the door of her aunt's studio. Aunt Nell was sleeping soundly. She tiptoed through to the kitchen and opened the refrigerator door.

Aunt Mollie had outdone herself. The shelves were full, just as Lynette had said.

Bonnie put a little bit of everything on her plate. It was delicious. At the rate she was going, Bonnie decided, she would probably gain at least ten pounds before she got home.

The phone rang.

Bonnie pounced on it before it could ring a second time and wake Aunt Nell.

"Could I please speak with Nell Boone?" a man's voice asked.

Bonnie hesitated. "She can't come to the phone. Could I take a message?" she said.

"This is John Oliver, with Armstrong Security Systems. Mrs. Boone contacted us about installing a system there. We've got everything in, finally, and we're just waiting for the word from her to come and install it."

"I know she's anxious to talk to you," said Bonnie. "In fact, I think she's been trying to contact you. Let me take the number and have her call you back."

"It's 555-SAFE," Oliver said. "We'd about decided she'd changed her mind."

"I'll give her the message," said Bonnie. She hung up the phone and made a note on the message pad hanging on the wall.

Bonnie rinsed her dishes and checked Aunt Nell again. She was *still* sleeping.

Bonnie scribbled a second note on the pad beside the phone that she and Lynette were at Marc's, then hurried to the museum.

As Bonnie came around the side of the building, she could see Lynette through the window sitting at the table holding a doll, a black doll.

Bonnie quietly slipped inside the museum and stood at Lynette's shoulder.

When Lynette didn't say anything, Bonnie cleared her throat.

Lynette dropped the doll and pushed away from the table, almost knocking Bonnie down.

"You scared me!" she said.

"I'm sorry," Bonnie apologized. "Really." She picked up the doll Lynette had dropped and began to examine it. "Where'd you get this?"

"I made it," Lynette said very softly.

"You? *You* made it? It's wonderful!" said Bonnie. She thought it was even better when she learned Lynette had made it herself.

"My grandmother taught me a lot before she died, and Mrs. Boone has been working with me since then," said Lynette. "Do you really think it's good?"

"I thought you'd found one of the slave dolls," Bonnie said.

"I used the picture in the book as a guide."

Bonnie heard the museum door open, and looked around.

"Anybody home?" Marc asked as he entered.

"Look, Lynette made this." Bonnie held the doll up for Marc to see.

He set down the kitten he had carried inside and took the doll.

The cat immediately rubbed against Bonnie's legs, then Lynette's.

"Not bad, Lyn," said Marc.

"It's like the doll in your grandfather's book," said Bonnie.

"I'm not completely finished yet."

Marc tossed the doll to Lynette who caught it, then gave him a dirty look.

"I've seen you play ball. I knew you'd catch it," he said.

"How did you get out for the night — What did you tell your grandfather?" Lynette asked Marc.

"That I was coming over to Mrs. Boone's to see you girls. By the way, here's your bandage." Marc tossed a pinkish-brownish ball at Bonnie.

She missed and it rolled across the floor with the kitten close behind.

"I don't play ball," Bonnie said. She picked up the bandage.

"Sit down and I'll show you how to wrap it," said Marc.

Bonnie reluctantly sat in a folding chair and removed her tennis shoe.

Marc wrapped her ankle quickly and expertly.

"Thanks," said Bonnie, slipping her shoe on before Marc had a chance. "It feels better."

"What are we going to do all night?" asked Marc.

"I'm worried about staying out all night," said Bonnie. "We won't be able to turn the lights on. If we do, won't Aunt Nell and Aunt Mollie see them and wonder what's going on down here?"

"We'll have to go back up to the house, then slip back down after your aunts are asleep. If we do that, they won't see the lights. I'm not even sure they could see the lights all the way down here anyway," said Lynette.

Bonnie still wasn't sure she wanted to stay in the museum all night. She started to say something, but Lynette interrupted.

"It's the only way we can make sure nothing else happens," Lynette said.

"Let's put some of the shelving together, as long

as we're here," Marc suggested. "Later we can tell ghost stories."

"Your aunt Mollie said if one more thing happens, Mrs. Boone is going to forget about the museum," said Lynette.

"Aunt Nell? Give up? Last night that was the last thing on her mind. She said nothing would keep her from opening, *and* on time," said Bonnie.

"She's evidently changed her mind, according to Mrs. Snyder."

"Which we don't know for sure because Aunt Mollie won't let us in to see Aunt Nell."

"If nothing else happens, we don't have to worry about it anyway," said Lynette. She suddenly became quiet and walked to the window looking out over the cemetery. "Shh!" she said. "Turn out the lights."

Before either Bonnie or Marc could reach the switch, the lights went out, plunging the museum into darkness.

# 10

Bonnie heard a crash as Marc dropped the shelves he had been working on. "Marc? Lynette? Where are you?" she asked, stumbling in the direction of the crash.

"I'm over here," Marc said. "Why'd you turn the lights out before we had a chance to find the flashlight?"

"I didn't," said Bonnie. "They just went out. It was like magic. Lynette said to turn off the lights and they went off."

"Then a fuse must have blown," said Marc.

Bonnie walked in the direction of Marc's voice. "Keep talking to me," she said, "so I can find you." She felt the front door open. "Who's there?" Bonnie called out. No one answered her.

Bonnie reached her hand into the darkness, hoping to find Lynette or Marc. "Lynette, talk to me," she said. She could hear someone else moving around, knocking into things. The tiniest sliver of light appeared and Bonnie could see Mark was holding onto a lighted match.

The circle of light suddenly grew. "Here's the flashlight," said Marc as he switched it on and moved the beam around the room. "Where's Lynette?"

"The door opened . . . ," said Bonnie. "Surely she didn't . . ."

They heard a scream from outside.

Marc ran out the open door. Bonnie followed behind, trying to keep up in spite of the pain in her ankle.

They heard another scream, muffled this time.

Marc aimed the flashlight in the direction of the noise. Down the hill, toward the cemetery, Bonnie saw a flash of white, moving toward them.

Marc ran down the hill.

Bonnie let him go, too frightened to follow. She looked at her aunts' house, with lights shining brightly and wished she were there.

"Lynette!" she heard Marc say. "What happened?"

Bonnie hobbled down to join Marc and Lynette as quickly as she could.

"I thought I saw someone moving around outside right before I asked you to turn the lights out. When you said a fuse must have blown, I wasn't so sure. I decided to go out and check the electrical box.

"When I got outside, I saw someone running around the corner of the building, from the back where the electrical box is. I started after the person, then got scared and started back.

"The next thing I knew someone threw this on top of me and shoved me down. That's when I screamed." Lynette held out a light-colored canvas tarpaulin.

"Who was it?" Bonnie asked, looking over her shoulder nervously.

"I didn't get any kind of look at all," said Lynette. "They looked big is all I can say for sure."

"They? It was more than just one person?" asked Bonnie.

"I just saw one person," Lynette said to Bonnie more than Marc. "Whoever it was had on dark clothes, slacks or pants. I would say a man."

*Someone big*, thought Bonnie, *an adult, in pants, a man. Dr. Allen*? She couldn't look at Marc. *Or was it one of the boys who kept driving by in that rusty car*. It was so dark out it could have been anyone.

"We'd better get back and fix the lights. I'll bet that someone switched off the main fuse box from the outside," said Marc.

Bonnie was first to head away from the cemetery.

She stepped inside the door of the museum.

"What are you children doing down here at this

time of the night?" Aunt Mollie's voice boomed out of the darkness of the museum's interior, scaring Bonnie half to death.

"Aunt Mollie!"

"You're supposed to be at Marc's," said Aunt Mollie, "but how can you be there when he's supposed to be at our house?"

Aunt Mollie's hat was pushed back on her head and her gold hair stuck out in all directions. She clutched her straw bag close to her side. "What was all that screaming about?"

"We're keeping a lookout, making sure nothing happens down here," said Bonnie.

"Well you're doing a poor job of it!" said Aunt Mollie. "What did you do to the lights? I've tried every switch and they won't come on."

Marc came inside. "It's not a fuse," he said. "Someone snipped the wires coming out of the electrical box."

"Someone did what?" Aunt Mollie said.

"Give me that flashlight," said Lynette. She walked around the entire room, shining the light over every surface. When she got to the table, she bent over and played the light on the floor underneath it.

"What?" asked Bonnie, joining Lynette.

"My doll is gone!" she said, her eyes bright with tears.

"Your doll? What doll?" asked Aunt Mollie.

"She was showing us a doll she had made," Marc explained.

"And it's gone!" said Lynette.

"All right, all of you get up to the house right now," Aunt Mollie ordered. "No more night watch for any of you."

Aunt Mollie brought up the rear as they climbed the hill to the house. She mumbled under her breath the entire time, but not loud enough for Bonnie to make out what she was saying.

"Where have all of you been?" Aunt Nell asked as soon as they walked in.

No one said a word.

"Mollie, you look a mess! What's going on?"

Lynette sat down beside Aunt Nell and started crying softly. "They took my doll," she said. "All the dolls at the museum and they took mine, the one I'd been working on all summer."

Aunt Nell reached out and drew Lynette closer to her. "All right, what's happened?"

"Someone got into the museum again," Aunt Mollie said. "They took some doll Lynette said belongs to her. Nothing else seems to be missing."

Aunt Nell turned pale and leaned back into her pillows.

"Lynette saw someone and chased them and they knocked her down," Bonnie said.

"Lynette! You aren't hurt, are you?" Aunt Nell hugged her tighter.

Lynette shook her head, burying it deeper into Aunt Nell's shoulder.

"And somebody cut the wire that feeds the electricity into the museum," Marc said.

"I can't let this put my family and friends in danger. As far as I'm concerned the museum is on hold," Aunt Nell said in a voice that made her sound worn out.

"Aunt Nell! You can't!" Bonnie jumped out of her chair and picked up a doll in each hand. "What are you going to do with all these dolls?"

"Bonnie, maybe Nell knows what she's doing. We've been contacted by lots of other museums. Maybe we should sell some of the dolls," said Aunt Mollie.

"You can't!" Bonnie said again. "Aunt Nell, these dolls are too important. You've spent your whole life with them. They're part of the family. Aunt Nell!"

"I'm not about to make any decision tonight," Aunt Nell said with little of her usual spark. "What did Scarlett O'Hara always say? 'I'll think about it tomorrow.' "

"You girls go on up to bed," Aunt Mollie said. "I'll stay down here with Nell tonight."

"Lynette?" Bonnie put her hand on Lynette's shoulder. "Do you want to sleep upstairs in my room?"

Lynette sat up. She nodded.

"You girls be quiet up there," Aunt Nell said.

"We promise you won't even know we're here," Bonnie whispered.

Marc, Lynette, and Bonnie tiptoed out of the room.

"Should I go on back to the museum and keep an eye on things?" Marc whispered.

"Marc, you get on home," Aunt Mollie said from the studio. "No one, I repeat, no one is to go down to that museum again tonight."

"I guess I'll go on home," Marc said.

"See you tomorrow," said Bonnie. "I'll let you out."

"Lock the door," Aunt Mollie called.

Bonnie turned the lock and tested the door.

As soon as they got to her room, Bonnie turned on the fan her aunt Mollie had given her that afternoon. Then, she opened the door to the porch.

Bonnie and Lynette stepped outside and leaned against the rail.

"The moon is beautiful," Lynette said. "Look at the path it cuts across the cemetery."

Bonnie shivered.

"What's wrong?" Lynette asked.

"Look at the way the moon picks out the mausoleum," she answered. "That's so spooky. Those people aren't really buried."

"I don't think it's spooky at all," Lynette surprised her by saying. "The family tomb is kind of special and it's not gross inside at all. It's kind of like a church."

"You're kidding? You've been inside?"

"I've been there with your aunt Nell. You really should go, too. If you did you wouldn't feel the way you do."

"Maybe I will, tomorrow," Bonnie said. "I'll think about that tomorrow."

# 11

"Geez, look at the time!" Bonnie rolled over and stuck her watch out to Lynette. "I can't believe we slept so late."

"It's so cloudy outside. That's why," Lynette said, then yawned. "A perfect day to sleep in."

"It's cooled off some, too, don't you think?"

"Still miss that air conditioner, don't you?" said Lynette.

Bonnie threw off the sheet. "What do you think Aunt Nell has on the schedule for us today?"

"Who knows? I just hope Mrs. Snyder made some more of those cinnamon rolls."

The girls dressed, taking turns in the bathroom. Bonnie carefully rewrapped her ankle. The swelling had all but disappeared.

"I don't think Aunt Mollie is around," Bonnie said as they went downstairs. "It's too quiet."

"No one is here!" Bonnie said when they got to the studio. "Where'd they go?"

Lynette crossed the hall to the kitchen.

"There's a plate of cinnamon rolls in here," she called out, "and a note."

"Gone to the doctor. Be back soon. Decided to let you girls rest. Just take it easy until we return. N.B." Bonnie read aloud.

"I think I'll change the sheets on your aunt's bed and straighten up the studio a little," Lynette said. "She hates it when it gets so messy."

"I was thinking of going to the cemetery, but I'll help you here. Maybe we can look around some more in those boxes we brought over from the museum, too," Bonnie said, feeling a little guilty she didn't think of straightening up her aunt's room.

"You go ahead and visit the cemetery. I think you should," said Lynette.

"Alone?"

"Once you get down there and see how interesting it is, you'll love it."

"I'll wait," said Bonnie. "You know the security company called last night, and I want to make sure and tell Aunt Nell. Maybe if she gets that installed, she'll change her mind about the museum."

"I can give her the message. Where is it?"

"On the notepad."

Lynette moved to the phone. "She must have found it already. It's not here anymore. There's no reason not to go to the cemetery this morning. And you'd better not wait. It looks like rain."

Bonnie reluctantly agreed. All she had to do was walk down there and run back.

"I promise you, it won't be that bad," Lynette said.

"You guys and that cemetery! I'm not going to get any peace until I go down there, I know that," said Bonnie.

"You're right," said Lynette.

Bonnie pushed away from the table. "If I'm gone too long, send a search party."

Lynette took hold of Bonnie's shirt collar and pushed her out the backdoor, making a great show of locking the door so Bonnie couldn't get back in.

Bonnie decided she would mosey down to the cemetery just like Margaret might have done over a hundred years ago. She could feel her long skirts swirling against her legs and hear the workers calling out to her as she passed by them.

Margaret would not have carried a parasol. And she would have climbed over the low stone wall rather than have gone to the gate.

Bonnie sat on the wall, pretended to gather her skirts, then swung her legs up and over to the far side. She slid to the ground.

"Hi!"

Bonnie heard a voice coming from behind a tombstone. She couldn't move.

"You look like you've seen a ghost," said Marc, popping out from behind a carved monument.

Bonnie leaned against the wall, weak with relief that it was a real person walking toward her between the rows of tombstones.

"I've been to the museum already," he said, joining her. "There isn't anything else missing, from what I could see. Your aunt Mollie must have saved the day."

"Did you get into trouble with your grandfather?" Bonnie asked.

"He wasn't even there. He gets called out all the time for emergencies," Marc said.

So Dr. Allen wasn't at home when the doll was taken. She'd have to remember to tell Lynette.

"I'm glad you're here. I want to go look at the mausoleum, but I didn't really want to go alone," Bonnie confessed.

She felt a drop of rain hit her arm, then another, then another. "Oops, guess we'll have to make it another time. It's raining," Bonnie said.

Marc took her hand and started toward the tomb. "We can wait out the rain either under the dome or inside the mausoleum," he said.

Bonnie held back.

"Come on." Marc jerked her forward. "I'll tell you a story. About Margaret."

"The dome," Bonnie said quickly. "Under the dome." She wanted to hear about Margaret. Bonnie was beginning to feel as though there was a bond between them.

It was raining harder. Marc ran and Bonnie ran after him.

When they reached the dome, Marc drew Bonnie up a short flight of steps and under the gray, stone, arched roof. He sat down, pulling his knees close to his chest and resting his chin on them.

Bonnie settled herself against one of the pillars. The orange kitten jumped up, curling itself in her lap.

"Where'd he come from?" Bonnie asked.

"He must have followed me over from the museum," said Marc. "He stays right there, outside the building, waiting for someone to feed him."

"We need to name him. And tell Aunt Nell about him."

"Where's Lynette?" asked Marc.

"She's doing some straightening up at the house."

"Did your aunt Nell ask her to stay in and help?" asked Marc.

Bonnie shook her head. "Aunt Mollie took Aunt Nell to the doctor's. Lynette thought it would be nice to straighten up Aunt Nell's room a little. I wish I'd thought of doing it."

"So she's there by herself?" said Marc.

Bonnie nodded, wondering about the strange tone in his voice.

"I hate to be the one to say this," said Marc.

Bonnie waited.

He didn't go on.

"Hate to say what?" she finally asked.

"It's about all the trouble at the museum and Lynette." Marc picked up a leaf and rolled it into a cylinder. "Has she said anything to you about some old dolls that your aunt won't admit are missing?"

"The black dolls, from the Civil War," said Bonnie.

"Right. Did she seem to be kind of upset with your aunt?"

"A little. But she plans to find the dolls. I'm going to help."

"Bonnie, she's more than a *little* upset. I'm worried that maybe she's trying to get back at your aunt."

Bonnie couldn't believe her ears. Marc thought Lynette was behind all the trouble.

Just then Lynette ran up the steps to the domed porch, shaking water out of her hair. "I'm soaked," she said.

Bonnie's and Marc's eyes met. She would swear she heard his teeth click together he shut his mouth so suddenly.

"Marc was just getting ready to tell me a story about Margaret," Bonnie said quickly.

Lynette sat down and leaned against one of the

marble pillars. "Go ahead," she said, reaching over to pat the kitten.

Bonnie shifted slightly, trying to find a more comfortable position on the hard stone floor. The kitten raised his head and gave her what Bonnie interpreted as a dirty look. "Okay, I'll sit still," she said to him.

Bonnie waited for Marc to begin.

"Margaret Scott, my grandfather says, was a beautiful woman and an unusual woman for the time she lived in," Marc said.

"She had a career. With the help of some of the servants — "

"Slaves," Lynette corrected.

"Okay, slaves," he amended. "She built up a thriving doll business. Margaret was a very talented artist and soon was specializing in portrait dolls, dolls sculpted to look like real people.

"The Allens were the family across the road. The father was a doctor, very successful, and he had three sons grown or almost grown, and a very young daughter who wanted a doll that looked just like her.

"Dr. Allen couldn't say no to his little girl, but he couldn't imagine asking a Scott to do anything for him, especially anything that involved slave labor. You see, Dr. Allen was an ardent abolitionist.

"Thomas, the oldest son, was also very fond of

his little sister and decided he would get her the doll regardless.

"He talked to Margaret. She agreed. He talked to her again and again and again. They were talking about this doll everyday. Then Thomas announced he and Margaret were in love and planning to marry."

"Oh, no," Bonnie said, remembering the portrait of Colonel Scott and those cold, blue eyes.

"The war broke out. Colonel Scott went off to join the Confederate forces and fight for the South, but one of his last acts was to forbid Margaret and Thomas' marriage."

"Poor Margaret!" said Bonnie.

"See that headstone over there?" Marc pointed through the curtain of rain.

Bonnie tried to figure out where he wanted her to look.

"The one with a horse on it," Marc said.

Bonnie found it quickly. It was the one she'd seen on her first trip to the cemetery, the one on the cover of Dr. Allen's book.

"Thomas was riding through this cemetery one night on his horse and he was shot, by a sniper. The site of his grave is also the site of his murder. It's rumored he was a conductor on the Underground Railroad and that's why he was killed, but it's only a rumor," Marc said.

"And Margaret never married," said Bonnie.

"She became *very* famous, but no, she never married."

Lightning tore through the sky, the wind picked up, and thunder boomed overhead.

Bonnie scooted closer to the center of the dome to escape the blowing rain. She tried, unsuccessfully, not to disturb the kitten. He uncurled himself from his place on Bonnie's lap and stretched, then lay down in Lynette's lap not even bothering to give Bonnie a backward glance.

"Maybe we should go inside," Lynette suggested as the wind bent trees and drove the rain harder.

"We'll get soaked if we try to run back to the house," said Bonnie.

"Not inside the house," said Lynette. "Inside here." She pointed down, under the floor below the dome.

Marc and Lynette got up. They went down the steps, then disappeared behind them. Bonnie followed.

She found herself staring at a pair of bronze doors.

Marc pulled on the doors until they opened.

There was a second set of stairs leading down into darkness.

"That's the burial vault, right?" Bonnie said.

Marc nodded.

Bonnie started forward tentatively. She stopped.

"Let's just wait right here," she suggested.

"You need to see this," said Lynette.

She and Marc went inside.

Bonnie took a deep breath and followed. As her foot touched the last step, the upstairs doors slammed. At the same instant, darkness enveloped her.

She turned and ran back up the stairs in a fraction of the time it had taken her to go down.

Bonnie pushed against the doors with all of her might.

They would not open.

# 12

"Marc! Lynette!" Bonnie screamed. "Come help!"

Marc shoved Bonnie aside gently and shook the doors. "Darn," he muttered. "The wind must have slammed them hard enough to engage the lock."

Bonnie clutched Marc's arm. "What are we going to do?"

"Does anyone know you came down here?" Marc asked.

Bonnie shook her head.

"Does anyone know where you are?" Marc asked again.

The dark, Bonnie realized. Marc couldn't see her and she couldn't see him! "No," she finally said.

"Lynette, did you leave a note or anything?"

"I thought we'd be at the museum," Lynette said.

Marc sat down on the top step. "Somebody will find us, eventually."

"It's so dark in here," Bonnie said.

Marc stood up.

Bonnie heard coins clinking. A small — very small — beam of light broke the darkness, Marc's pockets to the rescue.

"I have this little flashlight, but I don't know how long it will last. I haven't ever changed the battery." Marc switched the light off.

"I didn't want to come here," Bonnie said.

Marc went down the stairs. Bonnie heard him moving around. She could even make out his form as her eyes adjusted to the absence of light.

"Here's Margaret," Marc said. He shined the penlight on a bronze plaque.

Bonnie stood up and reluctantly entered the chamber.

"I'll bet this sculpture was from some of her own work," Marc said, moving the light around so Bonnie could see Margaret's face cast in bronze.

Bonnie stroked the smooth, cool metal with her fingers, exploring each feature.

She felt a tickle around her ankle and shook her foot to get rid of it. When she did, a small, furry ball scampered away, yowling.

Marc's light danced madly around the room. "It's the cat," he said, laughing.

He moved away from Bonnie, following the cat.

Bonnie gulped in air. She felt like it was all being swallowed by the blackness surrounding her.

The light came to rest against a rough, plaster wall behind the steps.

Bonnie moved through the darkness carefully, not wanting to let Marc get too far away from her.

As she approached, the cat arched its back and hissed.

Bonnie reached out to pet the cat, trying to calm him.

It backed away.

She watched as the cat turned and seemed to disappear into the wall.

"It's gone," said Marc, amazement evident in his voice.

Bonnie and Lynette squatted beside him.

"Marc . . ." Bonnie said, touching the cracked plaster in front of her. She found the gap the cat had slipped through, stuck her fingers in the opening and felt wooden planks. The plaster crumbled at her touch. When she had cleared through to the boards, she grabbed onto the wood, tugging gently. It made a creaking noise.

"There's something behind here," Bonnie said. "Help me get this board loose."

Marc pulled with her and it came away easily. He shined the light in the opening.

Bonnie stuck her head in and looked around. The kitten sat in the middle of a dirt-lined tunnel, washing its paws. When the cat noticed Bonnie, it stopped its bath and scampered away, vanishing into the dark beyond.

"What's back there?" Lynette asked.

"It's a tunnel," Bonnie said, pulling her head out. "It's mainly dirt, but it looks like there might be some wood holding it up."

She started chipping away more plaster and tore another board off to make the opening wide enough to climb through.

"A tunnel," Lynette repeated. "The tunnel is *here*?"

Bonnie freed a second board and started on a third.

"Help me," she said. "This one is stuck."

Marc and Bonnie wrestled with the stubborn wood. It groaned loudly and loosened slightly, but wouldn't pull away.

"I still can't fit under here," said Bonnie, lying face down on the floor. She moved out of the way. "Lynette, you're skinny. You try."

Lynette leaned down and looked inside the tunnel. She looked at Bonnie. "Why can't you fit?" she asked.

"I'm too fat," Bonnie answered.

Marc burst out laughing.

Bonnie glared at him.

"You are not," he said.

"Just watch. If I get stuck, it's *your* fault." Bonnie flopped down on her stomach and poked her head through the opening. She inched forward slowly expecting any moment to find herself stuck. Without even touching the wood, Bonnie made it through to the other side. She looked down at her body, then at the hole. She *was* small enough to fit through.

Lynette followed, having to work a little to fit herself through.

"I still can't get through," Marc yelled after them.

In the tunnel, Lynette turned around. Sitting, she raised her legs.

"Move back!" she called to Marc.

Lynette waited. "Are you out of the way?" she asked.

"What are you doing?" asked Marc.

"Just get out of the way."

Lynette kicked against the wood with her feet once, then twice. The third thrust sent the board flying.

"Great legs!" said Marc, crawling through the opening on all fours.

"Years of playing softball," Lynette said. "Despite what everyone thinks, you do have to run a lot."

"Give me the light," said Bonnie.

Marc handed it over.

Bonnie flashed it around the tunnel. The walls and floor were packed dirt reinforced at intervals with rough hewn beams.

She started to crawl forward carefully.

"You know what?" Bonnie heard Lynette say. "If I'm not completely turned around, I think we're going in the direction of the museum. Maybe this leads to the room where we found the kitten in the first place. He seems to know where he's going."

Bonnie had no idea what direction they were going. But Lynette might be right. Wouldn't this be a story to include in her history project? Afraid that the light wouldn't last much longer, Bonnie switched it off and felt her way ahead with her hands and knees. The floor seemed to slope slightly.

Eventually, Bonnie could stand up.

She touched a solid surface before her. "We're there," she announced to Marc and Lynette. "I think we're at the museum."

Bonnie turned the light on. The tunnel ended at a door. She grasped the metal handle and tugged on it.

The door creaked open.

# 13

Bonnie let the thin beam of light play around the room. Disappointment and excitement warred within her. The tunnel did not lead to the empty room under the museum. They were still trapped. However, the stone-walled room she entered slowly was far from empty.

Benches lined the walls. On the benches sat rows of dolls.

"Lynette, your dolls!" Bonnie managed to say.

The flashlight dimmed and sputtered.

"Uh-oh," said Marc, "not a good sign."

"Maybe there's something in here we can use as a light," said Bonnie.

"I don't think we're going to find electricity, Bonnie. This place smells like it's been closed up for a long, long time," said Lynette.

"A candle then or a lantern," Bonnie said. "There must be something!"

Bonnie ran the dimming light over the benches.

"I've got it!" she heard Marc shout.

She turned around.

"A candle!" He held up a squat, white stub.

"What good is a candle — "

"Without matches," said Marc. He held them up.

"What else do you carry around in your pocket?" Lynette asked him.

"Hey, what can I say? I'm a Boy Scout."

A glow of light grew from across the room as Marc held the candle high.

"Where did all these dolls come from?" he asked.

"I think they must be some of the black dolls your grandfather mentions in his book," Bonnie said. "Margaret and the slave women made them."

Bonnie picked up one of the dolls and examined it. She recognized the rough cotton dress as the same type of dress that she and Lynette had discovered in the box at the museum.

"Marc, move the candle closer so I can see this better."

"No, move it over here," said Lynette.

"There's only one candle," Marc said. He moved over beside Lynette.

Bonnie watched as Lynette picked up one doll after another.

"I always knew they were somewhere," Lynette said. She cleared a spot on the bench and sat down, surrounded by dolls.

Bonnie picked one up. She felt a hard lump under her fingers.

Moving into the small circle of light the candle made, Bonnie pushed back the doll's shift. Underneath she found a red cotton heart sewed onto the doll's chest. Something crackled inside. She remembered something about hearts. The dolls that appeared when a slave escaped had hearts; Margaret's dolls didn't.

Bonnie carefully removed a square of yellowed paper, unfolded it, and tried to read it.

"Hold the candle steady," she said to Marc. The wavering light made the faded script even harder to decipher.

"This is amazing! Listen. 'Daisy. Freed from Oak Crest Plantation, Mississippi. March 23, 1862. Arrived in Callaway May 31, 1862. To Ohio June 11, 1862.' Then there's a little M.S. embroidered on the heart."

Bonnie laid the doll down and picked up a second, this one a male. Under his shirt she found the same red heart.

" 'George. Freed from Dickson Plantation, Louisiana,' " Bonnie read. "And there's a date and the initials M.S. again."

She picked up another doll and another. Each one had a red heart and a slip of paper with a name, a place, a date, and a set of initials. Sometimes the initials were M.S.; on others Bonnie found an R.S.

Bonnie reached out for another doll. This one felt different. The dress was softer and was much fuller. Bonnie pulled the doll into the candlelight.

"Marc, Lynette, look. It's Margaret — in a wedding gown."

Bonnie moved along the bench beyond the spot where Margaret had rested.

Marc followed her, holding the candle.

Bonnie picked up a doll dressed in the uniform of a Union soldier and held it out to Marc.

"Thomas?" she asked.

Marc nodded, taking the doll.

"Maybe they planned to marry anyway," said Bonnie.

Marc just shrugged.

"The tunnel, this room — it was all part of the Underground Railroad, wasn't it?" said Bonnie, needing to say the thoughts that were careening around inside her head and make them real.

"And M.S. must stand for Margaret Scott. She made a record of the people she helped escape by creating a doll and sewing its secret in a little heart. She fooled people by not putting hearts on her other black dolls."

"R.S. . . . That must be my great-grandmother, Rosa Scott. She was involved, too," said Lynette, closely examining one of the dolls marked with the initials R.S.

Bonnie lifted up Margaret's wedding gown and found a tiny heart embroidered with an R.S. The inside of the heart was empty. "Rosa must have made this for Margaret, maybe a wedding present for a wedding that never happened."

The light faded as Marc walked around the room holding the candle close to the walls, looking carefully, high and low.

"I still wonder if there isn't a way between here and the museum. The cat made it into that room under the museum somehow," he said.

"Which wall would be in the direction of the museum?" asked Lynette. "That's where we should concentrate."

"Over here, I think," said Marc.

"There doesn't seem to be a door, so look for different stones, loose stones," suggested Bonnie.

"Here!" Marc said triumphantly. "The stones are different here."

Bonnie looked for herself. They were rounder, smoother than the other stones lining the wall. Near the floor she found a small opening where two of the stones had come loose. "Here's something," she said. "Did either of you happen to notice if the wall of the storage room is anything like these stones?"

"I think it was," said Lynette.

"Let's try to get more of these stones free and see if this goes through to the museum," said Marc.

"This little hole is about right for a cat," remarked Bonnie. "And it's so low we maybe didn't notice it."

"Maybe we could tie a note on the cat and send it out for help. If we could find it," Lynette said.

Bonnie started to dig at the loose mortar. It was surprisingly easy to get out.

Slowly Marc, Lynette, and Bonnie chipped away, steadily enlarging the opening.

As soon as it was big enough, Bonnie poked her head through the hole. "We *are* under the museum," she said.

"Margaret must have closed up the tunnel at some point," said Bonnie. "Think what her father would have done if he'd found out. I wonder what Aunt Nell is going to say when she finds out?"

"My grandfather is going to be very happy. He's been looking for proof like this for a long time," said Marc.

"I'm already very happy," Lynette said.

Bonnie looked down at her hands. They hurt, especially her fingers. She began to wonder if it wouldn't be better to wait for someone to come find them.

"Can you fit through there yet?" Marc asked.

Bonnie looked at the hole. It didn't look very big. "Maybe," she said.

Bonnie stuck her head through the hole a second time. She twisted and turned trying to get her shoulders to fit through.

"We need some grease," said Lynette, joking.

"I'll try to get a few more stones loose," Marc said.

"No," said Bonnie. "I can make it. Just give me a few more minutes."

She fit her right shoulder through, then stretched her right arm over her head and pressed into the floor. Bonnie inched slowly forward and at the same time rotated her body, slipping her left shoulder through.

Marc and Lynette cheered as the rest of her body slid through easily.

"I'll keep working to get the hole bigger. You go around to the cemetery and unlock the doors to the mausoleum. We can get out that way," said Marc.

Bonnie scrambled up the ladder and pushed against the cupboard.

It wouldn't open.

# 14

"The cupboard won't budge," Bonnie said.

"Oh no!" Lynette yelled.

Bonnie banged on the door with the palms of her hands. "Come on," she shouted. "Open up!"

"Bonnie?" She heard a muffled voice from the other side of the door. "Is that you?"

"Aunt Mollie? Help! We're trapped down here!" Bonnie called. "Push on the back wall of the cupboard," she said. "But wait until I get out of the way."

Bonnie lowered herself down the ladder a few rungs.

The door above swung open and light poured into the room.

Bonnie climbed out. She grabbed her aunt and hugged her.

"What in the name of creation?" Aunt Mollie said.

"We found a tunnel and a room and dolls.

C'mon." Bonnie tugged at Aunt Mollie's hand. "See for yourself."

Bonnie descended the ladder again.

Aunt Mollie came down more carefully. "I don't like this ladder," she said.

"Marc, Aunt Mollie's here. Move out of the way and let her see inside the doll room."

Aunt Mollie stuck her head through the hole they had managed to create in the stone wall.

Lynette held dolls for her to see.

"I never!" Aunt Mollie said. "When I heard a voice behind that wall I thought I was going crazy. I still feel that way."

"Bonnie, go up into the museum and get some tools and a flashlight," said Marc.

"I could just run over to the cemetery and unlock the door," said Bonnie.

"We need to open this up anyhow. It won't be hard with a hammer and chisel," said Marc.

Bonnie searched through box after box in the museum until she found the tools Marc had requested. She had to squeeze past Aunt Mollie to hand them to him.

By then, Marc had removed enough stones that Lynette could fit through.

"We got locked in the mausoleum, in the cemetery," Bonnie said to Aunt Mollie. "And a cat was there with us. It disappeared through some boards behind the steps and we found a tunnel.

"It led to the room with all the dolls. They're the black dolls. They represent runaway slaves, and this was part of the Underground Railroad," Bonnie said.

"The cat is curled up in here under a bench," Marc said. "We thought there might be a connection between the doll room and the room under the museum because we'd found the cat in there the other day. In fact, it was the meowing of the cat that led us to the room behind the revolving wall."

"And they seemed to be in the same direction," said Lynette.

"Besides, how many secret rooms can one place have?" Bonnie added. "It seemed to fit. And we were right!"

Aunt Mollie just shook her head.

Marc popped through the hole.

"We'll open it the rest of the way later. Let's go tell Mrs. Boone," said Marc.

"Get some of the dolls to show her," said Bonnie.

Marc reached through the opening and grabbed the nearest dolls.

Aunt Mollie examined each one carefully. Bonnie showed her the hearts, the initials, and the scraps of paper inside each one.

"Nell just isn't going to believe it," said Aunt Mollie.

"Come on. Come with us and we'll tell her," said Bonnie.

"I think I'd better stay here," said Aunt Mollie. "Now that these dolls are here, I'm really uneasy about the security. I'll stand guard and we'll move all the dolls up to the house later. You go ahead and tell Nell. After all, you were the ones who found them."

Aunt Mollie patted Bonnie's head.

"There's another way in through the mausoleum?" she asked.

"But the doors are locked," Marc assured her.

"I'll just sit tight right here and make sure they're all safe," said Aunt Mollie. "Nell just isn't going to believe it."

# 15

"Hurry!" Lynette urged, running the distance between the museum and the house.

"I'm a distance runner, not a sprinter," said Marc, lagging behind Lynette.

Bonnie didn't even try to keep up with them. Her ankle was still sore enough to make it hard to run.

By the time she reached the house, Aunt Nell had hobbled out of the studio into the hall on her crutches and was listening to Lynette tell all about the dolls. She didn't look like she quite believed it.

When she couldn't keep quiet another minute, Bonnie cut in, "Aunt Nell, these are the dolls Dr. Allen wrote about in his book.

"And, we found an Underground Railroad tunnel. You're just going to die when you hear this, but *Margaret* helped on the railroad."

Bonnie heard Aunt Nell's sharp intake of breath.

"Does your grandfather know about this?" Aunt Nell turned to Marc.

"No ma'am."

"Get him over here. He can help me get down to the museum. I've got to see this for myself."

Marc hurried out of the room to call his grandfather.

Bonnie showed her aunt the heart pockets and the record stored in each one.

"There's another Margaret doll, too. Marc told me how she fell in love with Thomas and how her father refused to allow them to marry. . . ."

"The Allens weren't any more enthusiastic about it than the Scotts," said Aunt Nell. She lowered herself to the steps and leaned her crutches against the wall.

"And look what happened. Margaret helping slaves escape and Thomas getting shot in the cemetery.

"Where's Mollie? She'll want to be in on all of this, too," said Aunt Nell.

"She's already down at the museum. She was afraid to leave the dolls there in case somebody decided to break in again," said Bonnie.

"She doesn't have to worry about that anymore. The sheriff called and said he caught a couple of hooligans stealing a car from a house right near here last night. They also had some boxes in the trunk that I think they may have lifted from the museum, from the way the sheriff described the contents to me. Of course, the boys won't admit to it, but Sheriff Richter thinks they probably caused most of the trouble we've been having at the museum."

"Was it those two guys in the car we saw the other day?" asked Bonnie.

"What boys?" Aunt Nell asked.

"Kenny Diamond and Tommy Bischoff," said Lynette.

"That's right," Aunt Nell said. "You saw them here?"

Bonnie nodded. "They drove by, honking and saying stuff. They also drove up beside me when I was looking in the window at Aunt Mollie's restaurant the first day I was here."

"A couple of troublemakers, but not really dangerous," said Aunt Nell. "The sheriff will want to know you two saw them hanging around."

"They did knock Lynette down last night," said Bonnie.

"But we don't have to worry about them anymore. They'll be out of the way for a while," Aunt Nell said.

Marc came back in the room. "My grandfather is out on a call. His nurse said she'd send him over as soon as he got back."

Bonnie tried to curb her impatience. She wanted to get back to the museum.

Lynette was sitting on the steps next to Aunt Nell, showing her the initialed hearts on the dolls she had brought over.

Marc came over and whispered to Bonnie, "There's no way your aunt is going to be able to get into that room for a while. She can't crawl through the tunnel or go down the ladder with that leg."

Bonnie looked at her aunt. She wouldn't put it past Aunt Nell to try, broken leg or no.

"Young man," Aunt Nell said to Marc. "I don't know if I have the patience to wait for your grandfather." She looked at Bonnie. "I don't think you do either."

Bonnie looked down at the floor.

"What about your wheelchair? We could push you over in that," Lynette suggested.

"We'd either have to go all the way around on the road or over the field. I don't think it would be that easy to push in either place. Besides, I don't need a wheelchair. You girls go on back to the museum and send Mollie here to drive me. Marc, you'll have to stay to help me into the car."

Bonnie looked up at Aunt Nell.

"You girls go on," Aunt Nell said. "I wouldn't be sitting here either if I had any choice." She sounded grumpy, but she was smiling.

Lynette ran and Bonnie hobbled back to the museum.

"I'm so glad we get to go back. I can't wait to see the dolls again," said Lynette.

"Aunt Nell took it pretty well, didn't she?" said Bonnie.

"She should be happy. She was already talking about what great publicity this will be for the museum," Lynette said.

"I never thought of that."

"You go on in here," said Lynette when they reached the museum. "I'll go open the doors to the mausoleum."

Bonnie entered the museum. "Aunt Mollie, I'm back!" She walked through to the cupboard.

"Aunt Mollie," she yelled again.

No one answered.

Bonnie climbed slowly down the ladder.

Aunt Mollie wasn't in the first room. Bonnie stuck her head through to the secret doll room.

Her aunt was sprawled on the floor. She didn't even move when Bonnie screamed.

# 16

Bonnie quickly squeezed through the opening to the secret room. She shook Aunt Mollie's shoulder. "Aunt Mollie, are you okay? Say something, please."

Lynette stumbled through the door leading to the tunnel. She stared at Aunt Mollie, openmouthed. "Is she . . . ?"

Bonnie felt for a pulse. It was throbbing strongly.

Aunt Mollie's eyelids fluttered. She moaned.

Bonnie sat back on her heels.

"What? What happened?" Aunt Mollie asked as she tried to sit up.

Bonnie touched her shoulder gently and pushed her back down. "When I came in, you were just lying there on the floor," she said, feeling greatly relieved that her aunt was talking again.

"I went back around and got the doors to the mausoleum open. Then I went through the mausoleum to the tunnel and pried some more of the boards away," said Aunt Mollie, her forehead wrinkled. "I heard the gates open behind me and I thought it was you. I said that I had made this opening a little bigger so that you could get to the museum through the tunnel without going all the way back around. Then I came back in here with the dolls, expecting you to follow me. But that's all I remember — until you found me here."

"It wasn't us that came in through the tunnel," said Bonnie. "You didn't see anyone?"

Aunt Mollie shook her head then winced. "I have a terrible headache."

"Whoever it was took the dolls," Lynette said. "I found this one in the tunnel. It must have been dropped."

Bonnie shined the flashlight over the benches. Margaret and Thomas were sitting where Bonnie had left them along with four or five black dolls. All the rest were gone.

"Maybe we should call the police," said Bonnie.

"Remember, your aunt Nell has already talked to them. She said the sheriff had called her. He picked up some kids who were trying to steal a car and he figured they were the ones who were messing around here," said Lynette.

"Yes, so if those boys are under arrest, then they weren't the ones who caused the trouble here *today*," Bonnie said. "Is the electricity fixed? Can we call the police from here or are we going to have to go back up to the house?"

Lynette felt around on Aunt Mollie's head. "I can't find any bumps. Did someone hit you?"

"I don't know," said Aunt Mollie.

"Did you smell something funny?" Bonnie asked, thinking someone might have used chloroform.

"Not that I remember," her aunt said.

"We'd better have Dr. Allen take a look at you," said Lynette. "He's on his way over here anyway to look at the tunnel."

"No!" said Aunt Mollie. "I'm fine, just a little headache. And no need to call the sheriff out here either. I don't like fusses."

Aunt Mollie stood up. She wavered for a moment, then sat down on the bench.

"I think we should get Dr. Allen over here," Lynette said to Bonnie in a low voice. "I'm still suspicious of him. He was out on a call, remember? I want to see what he does when he has to face your aunt. And the sheriff."

"We can't just accuse him," said Bonnie.

"No, but we can check him out," whispered Lynette. "See how he acts."

"Girls, I think I just need some fresh air," Aunt Mollie said.

"Can you climb the ladder?" asked Bonnie.

"I'll go out through the tunnel," said her aunt.

“We’d better take the rest of these dolls with us,” said Lynette. She raised the clothing of each of the black dolls. “None of these are Rosa’s,” she said.

“We’ll get the dolls back,” said Bonnie. “I know we will,” she said, not sure if she believed it or not.

# 17

Lynette and Bonnie hung back, letting Aunt Mollie walk ahead of them to the house after she insisted she was okay.

"I don't understand why Dr. Allen would take the dolls," said Lynette.

"I don't think he wants the dolls," said Bonnie, "or to hurt anybody." She looked at Aunt Mollie walking ahead of them, weaving every few steps. "From what you said he just wants his own museum and the town isn't big enough for two."

"But he's Marc's grandfather," said Lynette.

"I know. That bothers me, too," Bonnie admitted. "He seems so nice. He was the only one who really bothered about my ankle."

"What are you girls whispering about?" Aunt Mollie stopped to wait for them.

"Girl stuff," said Bonnie. She slipped her hand into her aunt's and squeezed. "I'm glad you're okay. You haven't given me one single recipe for my project yet."

"I've been working on it. You'll be real surprised when you see what I have for you. What was Lynette saying back there about Rosa's dolls?"

"Some of the black dolls have the initials R.S. embroidered on the heart sewed on their chest. We think it means that Rosa Scott, Lynette's great-grandmother, made the dolls. The others all have M.S. for Margaret Scott on them," Bonnie said.

"Does Nell know about the Underground Railroad?" asked Aunt Mollie.

Bonnie nodded.

"How'd she take it?"

"Pretty good, considering how she feels about Yankees."

They both laughed.

Lynette had gone on ahead and was already inside the house.

"Aunt Mollie, if we do find those dolls, I think the ones that Rosa Scott made should belong to Lynette. They really mean something to her. Besides, Aunt Nell keeps saying that I'm going to get all these other dolls someday just because I'm a Scott and my aunts and grandmothers and whoever made them. That's true for Lynette, too."

"We'll talk about it later, but I don't think I would get my hopes up about those dolls," said Aunt Mollie. "They're gone, remember?"

Aunt Nell, Marc, Dr. Allen, and Lynette were waiting in the hallway when Bonnie and Aunt Mollie walked inside.

"Lynette told us what happened. Are you sure you're all right?" Aunt Nell asked.

Bonnie didn't like the way Aunt Nell looked. Her face was white with a greenish tinge and her lips were quivering. Aunt Nell looked worse than Aunt Mollie, who had just been knocked out.

Dr. Allen immediately sent Marc out to the car to get his bag. He began the exam without instruments, asking Aunt Mollie to follow his finger as he moved it back and forth in front of her face.

"I told you I'm fine," Aunt Mollie said.

When Marc returned with the bag, Dr. Allen proceeded with a full examination, looking into Aunt Mollie's eyes, her ears, listening to her heart, taking her pulse, and measuring her blood pressure.

"If I were you, I'd go get an X ray of that head," said the doctor.

"Waste of money. I'll rest a while and be good as new by morning," said Aunt Mollie.

"You do seem to be all right," Dr. Allen admitted.

"Then I'll go fix us all a bite to eat." Aunt Mollie

headed down the hall toward the kitchen.

Bonnie ran after her. "We can feed ourselves. I like to cook, too, and I haven't had a chance to hardly walk into the kitchen since I've been here. Let us take care of you for once."

Aunt Mollie patted Bonnie on the head, then stroked her hair. "You're a real good girl," she said softly.

"Go on up to bed and I'll fix you a tray and bring it up."

Aunt Mollie hugged Bonnie tightly, then climbed the backstairs to her room.

Bonnie joined the rest of the group in Aunt Nell's studio.

"Maybe I'd better give up on the idea of the museum," Aunt Nell was saying when Bonnie entered the room.

"You can't do that," said Lynette.

"It does seem to be bringing lots of trouble your way," said Dr. Allen.

"Mollie and I are too old to be taking so much physical punishment. I didn't mind it when it was the museum itself that seemed to be the target, but I don't want my family in danger. What would Bonnie's parents do if something happened to her? Or Lynette's?" said Aunt Nell. "When the sheriff called to say he had those boys, I thought it was over, but it might be just beginning. You said some of the dolls were taken?"

"Most of them," said Lynette. "All of mine."

"You had some of the dolls you've been working on over in the museum, too?" asked Aunt Nell.

"I didn't mean mine really. I meant Rosa's," Lynette said.

"We'll have to call the sheriff," said Aunt Nell. "Mollie could have really been hurt, and the dolls they took are worth a lot of money. I hope whoever stole them realizes that and doesn't do anything that would damage the dolls."

"I'll talk to the police," Dr. Allen offered.

Aunt Nell looked grateful. "You can use the phone in the kitchen."

Dr. Allen left the room. Bonnie could hear his voice, but not his words.

"Sheriff Richter is coming by to talk to you and take a look at the tunnel. He also said he'd have the deputies step up the patrols a little tonight," said Dr. Allen.

"That's a little like locking the barn door after the horse is stolen, but I appreciate his concern. He told me he was already patrolling this area more often," said Aunt Nell.

"If you don't mind, I'd like Marc to show me that tunnel," Dr. Allen said. "I've looked for it for so long. I probably walked right over it a hundred times."

"Shouldn't you wait for the sheriff to check it first?" asked Bonnie.

"You're probably right," said the doctor. "Maybe we can come back after dinner and have a look. Marc and I better leave you girls alone now to get some rest. I still can't get over Mollie. She was unconscious, you say?" said Dr. Allen.

Bonnie and Lynette nodded.

"She certainly is one brave lady," said Dr. Allen.

"I'll fix you two some dinner if you want to stay," Bonnie offered.

"No, we have dinner waiting up at the house, but thanks anyway," said Dr. Allen.

"Call me if you need anything," he said to Aunt Nell.

Bonnie followed them out to the car. She peeked inside the backseat, but there was only a jacket and a pair of tennis shoes lying on the floor.

Marc opened the trunk and tossed the black bag inside.

Bonnie positioned herself to get a look in there, too. All she saw was a spare tire and a tool kit. No dolls.

# 18

The sheriff, a much younger man than Bonnie expected, arrived soon after Dr. Allen drove away. He talked to the girls and to Aunt Mollie, then went down to have a look at the tunnel and the museum. He assured Aunt Nell they would do everything they could to find whoever had injured Aunt Mollie.

After the sheriff left, Bonnie convinced Aunt Nell that she should rest for a while and let Bonnie fix everyone something to eat.

Lynette followed her into the kitchen.

"I took a look in Dr. Allen's car as he was leaving and it was empty. You know I've been thinking, whoever took the dolls must have hidden them someplace between the house and the cemetery," Bonnie said, whispering so no one could overhear.

"Why would they do that?" asked Lynette.

"Time," said Bonnie. "No one would have had enough time to sneak in, knock Aunt Mollie out, gather up all the dolls, and get away. Also, it would look awfully suspicious to carry a big bunch of dolls out of a cemetery. That means whoever took the dolls will have to come back and get them."

Lynette seemed to be thinking for a minute. She finally nodded. "But where did they hide them and when do you think they'll come back?"

"After we get finished with supper and Aunt Nell and Aunt Mollie are all settled, we'll go look. If the dolls are hidden, whoever took them will probably come back tonight, when it's dark."

"Your aunts will never let us out after this," said Lynette.

"They won't know."

"I wish we could take Marc with us."

Bonnie shook her head. "We just can't."

All the time she was talking, Bonnie was taking fresh vegetables out of the refrigerator and chopping them up.

"What are you going to make?" asked Lynette.

"Stir fry. It's easy and light. I don't think anyone wants anything too fancy," said Bonnie. She searched through the cabinets for a pan she could use to fry the vegetables. She didn't have any hope that Aunt Mollie owned a wok. Bonnie finally settled for a large iron skillet.

To her surprise, Aunt Mollie had some peanut oil in the pantry. Bonnie poured the oil in the skillet, let it heat, then dumped the vegetables and spices in. After a short time, she removed the skillet and divided the vegetables into four servings.

Lynette tasted a piece of broccoli. "Not bad, Scott," she said.

"We need trays and something for them to drink," said Bonnie.

Lynette pulled out two trays with legs and fixed glasses of tea.

They placed the plates and glasses on the trays and carried them to the hall.

"You take Aunt Nell's. I'll take Aunt Mollie's," said Bonnie. She started up the back steps.

The staircase was much steeper and narrower than the one that led up to the front bedrooms. The room at the top of the steps was fixed up like a living room with a couch, a TV, a recliner, and lots of books. Bonnie liked it.

"Aunt Mollie," she said softly.

"In here, darlin'," her aunt answered.

Bonnie crossed the living room and went into her aunt's bedroom. The room was smaller than the room she was staying in. It had one narrow window that looked out over the driveway. A ceiling fan whirred away overhead, making not a lot of difference to the room temperature.

It was so hot, Bonnie wondered how Aunt Mollie ever slept.

The room was furnished with a single metal bed, a dresser, and a large piece of furniture that Bonnie supposed was used to hang clothes inside.

Aunt Mollie stuck whatever she was writing under the afghan she had spread over the bed and held out her hands for the tray.

"Aren't you a little angel?" she said, sniffing the food. "It looks delicious."

Bonnie looked at her aunt carefully, trying to see if she was feeling any delayed effects from her bump on the head. She looked fine. She still had an appetite, too. Aunt Mollie was practically inhaling the food Bonnie had brought to her. She wasn't even taking time to talk.

"You must get this from me," said Aunt Mollie, pushing the empty plate away.

"Get what?"

"Your cooking. Nell doesn't like to talk about it, all she likes to talk about is dolls, but the women in our family are wonderful cooks. I'm going to prove it to you."

"How?" asked Bonnie.

"You'll just have to be patient. I'm not quite ready yet." Aunt Mollie leaned back against the pillows propped against the headboard of the bed.

"You tired?" asked Bonnie.

"Maybe a little." Aunt Mollie closed her eyes. "It's been quite a day."

Bonnie picked up the tray. "Lynette and I will

clean up the kitchen, so don't worry about that. You just get some rest."

"It's nice to have someone else doing the cooking for a change," said Aunt Mollie. "Nell thinks it's beneath her to even go in the kitchen."

"She's just busy with her own work," Bonnie said. "And maybe she thinks she might as well stay out since she couldn't possibly be as good as you."

Aunt Mollie smiled. "You're good for me, darlin'."

Bonnie wasn't quite sure what her aunt meant by that, but it sounded nice. She kissed Aunt Mollie on the cheek and left.

Lynette was already in the kitchen starting to wash the dishes. "It looks like the vegetables were a hit with Mrs. Snyder," she said.

"But not with Aunt Nell?" Bonnie noticed that the plate was almost untouched.

"She said she just didn't feel like eating. She wants me to save them for lunch tomorrow."

Lynette washed the dishes and Bonnie dried them. They worked in silence.

When everything was put away and the dish towels hung up to dry out, the girls tiptoed into Aunt Nell's study. She was asleep with the light still on.

Lynette turned the studio light off. She pointed up to Aunt Mollie's room.

Bonnie shook her head. She didn't want to take a chance on waking her aunt if she was already asleep. She motioned for Lynette to follow her upstairs.

They went out on the porch off of Bonnie's room and looked down at the cemetery. It wasn't quite dark yet. The stones were visible, but looked slightly blurred in the dusky light.

"Do you see anyplace that looks like a good spot to hide the dolls?" asked Bonnie.

"I think we're just going to have to look everywhere and hope we get lucky. We don't even know if they're there," said Lynette.

"They have to be," said Bonnie. "They just *have* to be."

# 19

Armed with flashlights and reeking of bug spray, Bonnie and Lynette walked slowly across the backyard toward the cemetery.

"If I'd just taken something and was worried that someone would see me before I could get rid of it, I don't think I'd come anywhere near the house," said Bonnie.

"Unless you thought that was what everyone would think," said Lynette, "so you'd do it anyway to fool them. My grandma always said the best place to hide anything was in plain sight."

"So you think we should start looking close to the house?"

"I think we should look everywhere, examine every inch of the graveyard," said Lynette.

"How about we start in the middle?" Bonnie suggested. "You go up toward the house and I'll go away from the house. We can cover a lot more ground if we divide it up."

"What if someone comes back to get the dolls?" Lynette asked.

"Then we'll know where they are," said Bonnie.

They climbed over the wall at the end of the yard.

Bonnie shined her light over the cemetery. She picked a row and pointed. "That looks like about halfway."

She walked down the row of tombstones, carefully playing her light over the ground. The name ALLEN was on several stones. Bonnie figured they must be related to Marc and his grandfather. She stopped when she came to a double headstone with the name Snyder cut into the stone. One side read

PETER
BELOVED HUSBAND OF MOLLIE
1926–1976

On the other side appeared

MOLLIE
BELOVED WIFE OF PETER
1937–

The thought that Aunt Mollie already had her name carved on a tombstone gave Bonnie the creeps.

She moved on. The rows were long. Bonnie had

gone up and down three of them and had not seen anything that would even suggest a hiding place. She looked around for Lynette.

Night had deepened and all she could make out of her friend was the beam of the flashlight. Bonnie looked up through the trees that shaded the cemetery by day. The stars twinkled and danced through the deep blue-black sky just like the fireflies that buzzed around Bonnie.

She turned around to check the house. The only lights burning were the ones they had left on in the kitchen and upstairs in their rooms. She turned a little farther around. The museum lights were blazing.

Quickly, Bonnie made her way to Lynette.

"When did the electrician come to fix the wiring at the museum?" Bonnie asked.

"I think he was there just as the sheriff was leaving," said Lynette.

"Somebody forgot to turn off the lights. Look." Bonnie pointed at the building. "We'd better go do it and make sure the door is locked, in case they forgot to do that, too."

Lynette switched off her flashlight as they walked toward the stone building.

"I guess whoever took them could have decided to stash the dolls someplace in the museum," said Bonnie.

"We can check it out," Lynette said.

The front door was open just a crack. Bonnie slowed down and let Lynette go up the steps ahead of her.

Lynette pushed the door open.

"It looks empty," said Bonnie.

They walked inside. The orange cat was sitting in the window looking out. It glanced at them momentarily, then resumed its watch.

Bonnie went over and petted him.

"Do you think we should check the tunnel?" asked Lynette. "I found one doll down there."

"At night? In the dark?" Bonnie said.

"It's always dark down there."

"I know, but it just seems scarier to think about going down there now. Besides, I don't think there's any place to hide anything in the tunnel."

Bonnie tried to follow the cat's line of vision to see if he was really watching anything or just staring out at the night in general. A tiny blob of light seemed to be moving through the cemetery.

She squinted, hoping it would become clearer.

"Lynette, come here a minute."

Lynette joined her.

Bonnie pointed to the light.

"Somebody's out there," Lynette said.

"Do you think we can sneak back down to the cemetery without using our flashlights?" asked Bonnie.

"We can try. But I have a better idea. If we go

through the tunnel, we can use our flashlights, we'll get there faster, and there's no way anyone will know we're coming until we actually get there," Lynette said.

Bonnie didn't like the idea of going into the tunnel any better even though there was a good reason to do it. She had a funny feeling in her stomach. She stared at the light bobbing through the cemetery.

"We don't know who it is out there," said Bonnie. "But if it's who we think it is, we need to make sure the thief doesn't get the dolls before we do."

The light was still moving through the cemetery.

"Why don't I sneak down toward the cemetery from the outside while you go make a quick check of the tunnel for the dolls. I'll meet you at the mausoleum," said Bonnie.

Lynette looked thoughtful. "That's not a bad idea. That way, if anything happens to one of us, the other one can go for help."

"Go for help! Thanks a lot. I really am anxious to go out into the dark by myself now," said Bonnie.

"We do need to remember what happened to Mrs. Snyder. And to me, too. I didn't just stumble and fall. Somebody pushed me out of the way last night," Lynette said. "But we can't just stay here and let someone get away with our dolls either."

"I know. Just look through the tunnel as fast as you can. I'll meet you at the other end," said Bonnie.

"Lock the museum door behind you," said Lynette, "and close the cupboard door. That way, no one will be able to come into the tunnel without our knowing it. You'll be able to see anyone heading that way anyway."

Bonnie watched Lynette descend the ladder into the room under the museum. She swung the back wall of the cupboard closed, then shut the cupboard door. At the museum door, Bonnie debated whether or not to leave the light on inside. She decided that she would. It might give her enough light to keep from falling over something outside and hurting her ankle again.

Bonnie walked slowly, trying to find the moving light again. It dawned on her that perhaps whoever held the light had spotted her and Lynette in the museum and had turned it off to sneak up on them. Bonnie froze. She listened to the darkness.

Leaves in the trees rustled. A bird swooped down, landed on a tombstone, then took flight again.

Bonnie walked a little farther into the cemetery. She listened again. This time she thought she heard the doors leading down to the crypt squeak.

She took several steps backward toward the safety of the museum, then stopped. She had to do this for Lynette, for Aunt Nell, for Margaret

The doors seemed to creak a second time, the sound magnified in the dark silence.

"It's just the wind," Bonnie whispered, trying to reassure herself.

Bonnie made an effort to relax. She straightened her shoulders, adjusted her shirt, and walked straight toward the domed mausoleum.

She tightened her grip on the flashlight. It would make her feel so much better if she could turn it on, but Bonnie knew there would then be no chance to surprise the thief.

Bonnie positioned herself in the middle of the floor under the dome. She turned slowly. She had no trouble finding the light, still now, in a row of graves a short distance away.

It was impossible to tell who held the flashlight or even if it was a man, woman, or child. Bonnie waited.

# 20

The light remained in place.

Bonnie tried to be patient, but soon tired of waiting for the light to come to her. She descended and began walking between the rows of headstones, purposefully heading away from the person with the light.

Bonnie was beginning to think the visitor had nothing to do with the dolls at all. Her confidence grew as she realized that whoever it was didn't even seem to notice she was there. She looked over her shoulder.

The light went out.

Bonnie stopped walking. She had a sense that the person was moving toward her. To be safe, she changed her direction.

She heard a squeak, the doors again. The light came back on, now appearing to come from the top of the stairs leading into the mausoleum.

Bonnie waited until the light disappeared, then

moved quickly to the tomb. She needed to warn Lynette.

She pushed the doors open wider, purposely making them squeak.

Bonnie listened to see if any noises were coming out of the crypt. She thought she heard a scraping sound, followed by a flop, flop, flop, like the sound of dirty laundry landing in a basket.

Bonnie entered the mausoleum and stood at the top of the stairs.

Even from where she was, Bonnie heard a gasp. She dared to peek at the intruder.

It was Aunt Mollie, her face so pale it practically shined in the darkness.

Aunt Mollie took a few stumbling steps forward. The basket she was holding fell to the ground and the dolls tumbled out.

"Bonnie?" Aunt Mollie whispered.

As Bonnie retreated, she could hear Aunt Mollie coming after her. She started to run.

# 21

Before she'd even made it out from under the steps, Bonnie's ankle was throbbing. She couldn't run very fast at all. Bonnie feared that even Aunt Mollie could catch up with her.

Bonnie raced between rows of tombstones finally reaching the stone fence. She tried to climb over, but everytime she had to put her weight on her ankle, a sharp pain shot up her leg. She ran along the fence looking for an opening.

She found one near the museum. Bonnie slipped through. By then, she couldn't see or hear Aunt Mollie. She quickly unlocked the door and ducked inside the building.

Bonnie tore open the cupboard door and pushed the wall out of the way. "Lynette!" she called out in a loud whisper. Bonnie hoped Lynette hadn't been trapped in the tunnel by Aunt Mollie.

Lynette scrambled up the ladder, heaving a

laundry basket full of dolls over the edge to rest at Bonnie's feet.

"I was sure she was going to catch you!" Lynette said. "I got to the mausoleum about the same time you did. When I saw Mrs. Snyder taking the dolls out, I couldn't move."

Bonnie nodded. "Aunt Mollie," she said, fighting tears. "Why would *she* take the dolls? She knows how much they mean to all of us." Bonnie sat down on top of a trunk that hadn't been removed yet, rubbing her ankle. "We need to get out of here. Aunt Mollie may show up any minute." She stood up. Her ankle wouldn't take her weight at all now. She should have rested like Dr. Allen said.

"You go ahead. Hurry. Take the dolls up to the house and tell Aunt Nell," Bonnie said. "Go, now."

"I can't tell Mrs. Boone that her own sister stole her dolls!" Lynette protested. "We can use the phone to call somebody. It should work now." She picked up the receiver, then froze.

Bonnie watched as Lynette's eyes grew larger and larger. She turned around slowly, afraid of what or who she might find behind her.

"You going to call Nell?" asked Aunt Mollie, who was standing in the front door. "This will break her heart."

Bonnie stood up and faced her aunt. "Why did

you take them, Aunt Mollie? Why?" Behind her back she motioned Lynette to slip away through the tunnel. Aunt Mollie couldn't go nearly as fast as Lynette could.

"You mean why *am* I taking them. Lynette, give me the dolls." Aunt Mollie held her arms out and walked toward Bonnie and Lynette. "You know, I almost found them myself. I found the first room under the museum, but I just didn't go far enough.

"I had a feeling about you, Bonnie, from the very first night, when we talked about the missing dolls. I knew if you stayed here long enough you'd find them."

Bonnie stood up, trying not to let Aunt Mollie see how much her ankle hurt. She stepped in front of Lynette. "Did you put that Margaret doll in my room the first night? And the note? Why? Were you trying to scare me into going home?"

Aunt Mollie nodded and looked pleased with herself. "I found the note the next morning, on the steps. I took it so Nell wouldn't see it. I knew she'd recognize my printing."

"Did you do everything: the fire, the broken windows, the paint, the table leg?" Bonnie asked.

"I didn't mean for Nell to get hurt," Aunt Mollie said. "I thought the table would collapse when she put something on top of it. She had no business climbing up on top of it. And I didn't mean for Lynette to fall last night when I pushed her. I just knew I had to do something to scare you kids off."

"But Aunt Mollie, someone hurt you this afternoon," said Bonnie.

"I was pretending. How else could I get away without anyone seeing me take the dolls?"

"I still don't understand why."

"Dolls, dolls, dolls. That's all I've heard my whole life. I was finally getting to do something *I* cared about, and the dolls took over again. Nell forced me to close my restaurant and help her out with the museum. We didn't have either the time or the money to do both and the museum would live on forever, she said. Of course, no part of me would live on with it, only the dolls and Nell.

"And then trying to make it all right by telling me I could open a little snack bar in *her* museum. She might as well have just stuck a knife in me. My skills don't mean a thing to her."

Aunt Mollie's face looked completely different as she lashed out against her sister. Bonnie had trouble believing this was the same woman who had been so kind to her — worrying about Bonnie's ankle and making doughnuts and cinnamon rolls for her. The woman talking to her tonight was angry, deeply angry, and it frightened Bonnie.

"I'm not asking for much. I'll take the slave dolls. That's all. I'm going to sell them and use the money to start a restaurant, another Mollie's, far, far away from Callaway."

"You'll never be able to sell the dolls. They're too distinctive," said Lynette.

"I'll be able to sell them all right. Not everyone cares where the goods come from as long as they're the real thing. But, for Lynette and for you, Bonnie, I am leaving Rosa's dolls. You're both right. Lynette should have her family dolls just like we have ours."

"Aunt Mollie, I don't want you to go away," said Bonnie, meaning it.

"I left you a little gift on the kitchen table. It might make you feel better, darlin'." Aunt Mollie smiled like her old self.

"Lynette, pick out the dolls with R.S. embroidered on the heart. I already have all the dolls you brought up to the house to show Nell earlier. I didn't want to leave anything behind."

A pair of car headlights suddenly lit up the museum.

Aunt Mollie pushed Bonnie out of the way and grabbed the basket.

Lynette held on tightly.

Car doors opened. Dr. Allen and Marc rushed through the door.

"What in the world?" said Dr. Allen. "Your aunt

Nell is worried sick about the three of you."

Aunt Mollie let go of the basket.

Lynette lost her balance and fell backward.

Bonnie waited for her aunt to explain what was going on.

"Mollie? Lynette? Bonnie?" said Dr. Allen, looking at each one of them in turn.

Marc held out his hand and pulled Lynette up. "Hey, you found the dolls!"

Lynette handed one of the dolls to Dr. Allen.

"It's just like the one in my book," he said. "This is wonderful, just wonderful. And the tunnel . . . I've looked for that for years. I knew it had to be here someplace and you kids found it just like that. They're pretty special, aren't they, Mollie?"

"Pretty special," Aunt Mollie said.

"So, what are you doing down here in the middle of the night? Your aunt woke up, found out you weren't in bed, and called me," said Dr. Allen.

"We realized we left the light on in the museum, so we came down to turn it off," Bonnie said, making up a fast excuse. She needed time to think what to do about Aunt Mollie. Bonnie looked to Lynette for help.

"Then we saw a light in the cemetery and decided to try to find out who it was," Lynette continued.

"It was me," said Aunt Mollie.

"She was visiting her husband's grave," Bonnie put in quickly, deciding this was a family matter. She didn't want anyone to get involved until she had a chance to talk to Aunt Nell.

"So once we were down here, we started looking around and we found the dolls stuck in a nook in the mausoleum," Bonnie said. "And then Aunt Mollie saw the light in the museum and she thought someone was up to no good."

"You could have gotten into all kinds of trouble down here alone," Dr. Allen scolded. "What if the person or persons who took the dolls came back here and caught you with them? They already assaulted both Lynette and Mollie. We don't know what they're capable of doing."

"We didn't think," said Bonnie. Knowing what she knew now, she realized she would rather have found real crooks than to have found out about Aunt Mollie.

"Go get in the car. I'll drive you back to the house." Dr. Allen held the door open for everyone to file out.

The doctor grabbed Bonnie's arm as she limped past him. "Is that ankle still bothering you?" he asked.

Bonnie nodded.

He knelt down and probed the ankle gently. "I think if you'll go home and put some ice on it and take a couple of aspirins, you'll feel better."

Bonnie felt tears burning her eyes. It was going to take more than that to make her feel better.

Dr. Allen patted her on the shoulder.

"Don't forget to turn off the light," said Lynette.

Outside, Aunt Mollie said, "I think I'll walk back. The fresh air will help me fall asleep." Without waiting for anyone to reply, she walked away.

No one said much on the drive back to the house. Lynette kept her arms wrapped around the basket, and Bonnie was too busy trying to figure out what to do about Aunt Mollie. What should she tell Aunt Nell?

"Thanks, Dr. Allen," said Bonnie as she got out of the car.

"See you tomorrow," Marc said as they drove away.

"Why didn't you tell him the truth?" Lynette asked.

"I couldn't. What would it accomplish anyway? We have the dolls," said Bonnie.

Aunt Nell threw the front door open. She hugged Bonnie then Lynette. "I was sure something had happened to the two of you. I can't believe you went running off again after what happened to Mollie. Where is Mollie anyway?"

"She wanted to walk home. She thought the

fresh air would help her sleep. We had a bit of excitement down at the museum."

"Excitement!" Nell exclaimed.

"Yes," said Bonnie. "We found the dolls."

Lynette held the basket so Aunt Nell could see.

"Glory be," said Aunt Nell.

# 22

Aunt Nell was in the kitchen alone the next morning when Bonnie finally came downstairs.

"Where's Aunt Mollie?" Bonnie asked.

"She's gone," said Aunt Nell, her voice sounding hoarse.

"When will she be back?"

"She won't be back for a while."

"Aunt Nell . . ."

"Mollie told me about what happened last night. We decided it would be better for her to go away for a while," Aunt Nell said.

"I guess you're really furious with her," said Bonnie.

Aunt Nell shook her head. "Just sad. I never knew how strongly she felt about things around here. The dolls have always been my life. I forget that that's not true for everyone."

"Did you tell the police?" asked Bonnie, still worried about Aunt Mollie.

"When Mollie said she was leaving, I decided that was punishment enough. I feel partly to blame for what happened."

"She's lived in this town her entire life. Where will she go?" Bonnie asked.

A tiny smile curved Aunt Nell's lips. "She said she might get a job cooking on a river barge or maybe even an ocean cruiser. She'd be good at it, too. Maybe someone will appreciate her cooking for a change."

"But she won't be here with us, her family," said Bonnie.

"What Mollie did was wrong," Aunt Nell said.

"Who's going to cook for you?" Bonnie asked.

Aunt Nell laughed. "I don't care much about what I eat. It was a waste for someone like Mollie to cook for me."

"What about the museum?" Bonnie asked.

"I'm going ahead with it, if that's what you mean. I may have to give in and take some Yankee help from that old rascal Ben Allen."

"I'll still be here to help, and Marc and Lynette."

"And I'm thankful for that," said Aunt Nell.

"I wish Aunt Mollie had at least waited to say good-bye," said Bonnie.

"That reminds me." Aunt Nell looked around the kitchen. "Pick up that blue notebook on the counter behind you," said Aunt Nell. "Mollie left it for you. I promised her I would give it to you."

Bonnie sat down at the table with the book in front of her. She opened the cover. On the first page, Aunt Mollie had printed The History of the Family Scott in Recipe, by Mollie Scott Snyder and Bonnie Scott.

She turned to the next page. The first recipe was for the colonel's cornbread. Bonnie knew who that must refer to. At the end of the recipe, Aunt Mollie had written that Colonal Seth Scott claimed that the only reason he made it home from the War Between the States was because he couldn't die until he'd eaten just one more piece of his wife's cornbread.

A recipe for wedding cake said that the cake had been served at every Scott daughter's wedding since 1904 when Beatrice McDutter Scott baked it for her daughter Kate's wedding.

The sponge cake recipe was attributed to Margaret Scott.

Pages and pages of recipes followed for every conceivable type of food. Each recipe had a story and Bonnie loved every one.

"I was thinking," said Aunt Nell, "you could include a picture of the doll that represents each family member beside their favorite dish. Don't you think that would really make the project special?"

Bonnie thought about it for a minute. She felt like smiling for the first time since she'd seen Aunt Mollie holding the dolls. If she included the pictures of the dolls along with the recipes, it would truly be a *family* history project.

She came around the table and gave Aunt Nell a hug. "Thanks to you and Aunt Mollie, this is going to be the best project ever," she said.

# 23

"Can you believe there are so many people here?" Bonnie whispered to Lynette. "I think the museum is going to be a real success."

Bonnie and Lynette were serving as hostesses at the opening of the Little Dixie Doll Museum. They were both dressed in costumes they had created from clothing stored in the attic. Bonnie was amazed that Lynette finally agreed to wear something other than a solid-colored T-shirt and denim shorts. Bonnie had made sure her outfit matched the clothing Margaret would have worn in the late 1800s. She made frequent trips to the display featuring the Margaret doll to hear comments by visitors on how much the young hostess looked like the doll.

Lynette stayed close to the display featuring the newly discovered black dolls. The exhibit also honored the contributions of the black slaves to the success of the doll business. Aunt Nell had even convinced Lynette to display one of her dolls.

Marc joined the two girls, carrying a cat in each hand. He was decked out in the full uniform of a Civil War Union officer. He bowed to Bonnie and Lynette.

"Can you do something with Tom and Maggie?" he asked. "I can't keep them away from the food."

Bonnie took Tom, the gold tiger cat. He'd quickly grown from the tiny kitten they'd found in the cupboard room into a large, friendly cat who was always hungry. Lynette took Maggie, a black-and-gold tortoise shell they had found wandering in the cemetery and adopted as company for Tom. Both cats made their home in the museum.

"They're honored guests," Bonnie said. "If it weren't for Tom we might never have found the dolls."

"You've got a point," said Marc. "We'll save them some of the leftovers. By the way, have either of you seen my grandfather?"

Bonnie pointed.

Near the front of the room, Dr. Allen hovered over Aunt Nell like a mother hen. He had taken up Aunt Mollie's museum responsibilities when she went away.

Bonnie missed Aunt Mollie. It had been a lot quieter since she'd gone away. Aunt Nell didn't say much, but Bonnie knew she missed her sister, too.

"Can I have your attention, please?" Aunt Nell asked the assembled guests.

"I have one more doll I'd like to add to the collection," Aunt Nell announced. "This doll honors the contributions of the most recent Scott daughter to our continuing tradition. Bonnie, will you please join me?"

Bonnie couldn't move. She'd expected to hear Lynette's name. She felt her entire body flush. She heard clapping all around. Blindly, Bonnie made her way to her aunt's side, still carrying the cat.

"The first day you came to Callaway, I explained to you that we had a tradition of creating a portrait doll in the likeness of each family member. Today, your last day in Callaway, I'd like to present Bonnie Scott." Aunt Nell held up a doll that was a perfect replica of Bonnie down to the freckles, long brown braid, designer T-shirt, and Keds tennis shoes.

Bonnie felt close to tears. Aunt Nell had been so busy. How had she found time to create such a wonderful doll?

"Many of you know the story of how Bonnie, with help from Marc Allen and Lynette Key, found the cache of slave dolls in the Underground Railroad room. In fact, Marc has probably coerced many of you to take a tour of the room and the tunnel. Dr. Allen has graciously set up a museum exhibit in the room honoring the efforts of both the North and the South during the War Between the States. If you haven't taken the tour, I urge you to do so.

"I want to publicly thank Bonnie, Lynette, Marc, and Ben Allen for all their help. Without them we might be standing in an empty room today."

The crowd laughed.

"Bonnie came here, reluctantly, to work on a family history project. She ended up teaching me a few things about our family. I'm thrilled we've had this time together.

"Would you like to say anything?" Aunt Nell asked Bonnie.

Thoughts about the summer rushed through Bonnie's mind. The family dolls, the museum, Lynette, the slave dolls, Marc, the cemetery, the mausoleum, the tunnel, Aunt Mollie. The happy times, the hard times.

Bonnie stepped forward. "Can I come back next summer?" she asked.

# About the Author

Like Bonnie in *Mystery of the Secret Dolls*, VICKI BERGER ERWIN enjoyed a large extended family when she was growing up. In fact, the great-aunts in the story are loosely based on members of her own family. And although none were doll makers, they were good cooks and talented quilters.

Ms. Erwin is also the author of *Jamie and the Mystery Quilt*. A University of Missouri graduate, she lives in Kirkwood, Missouri, with her husband Jim, their two children Libby and Bryan, and two cats.

APPLE®
Classics